TOP OF THE WORLD

AIR PIRATES OF CYRENAICA
BOOK THREE

BLAZE WARD

KNOTTED ROAD PRESS

Reviews
It's true. Reviews help. Even a short one, such as, "Loved it!" So please consider reviewing this book (and all of the ones you've read) on your favorite retailer site.

Never miss a release!
If you'd like to be notified of new releases, sign up for my newsletter.

http://www.blazeward.com/newsletter/

Buy More!
Did you know that you can buy directly from the Knotted Road Press website?

https://www.knottedroadpress.com/shop/

ALSO BY BLAZE WARD

The Jessica Keller Chronicles

Auberon

Queen of the Pirates

Last of the Immortals

Goddess of War

Flight of the Blackbird

The Red Admiral

St. Legier

Winterhome

Petron

CS-405

Queen Anne's Revenge

Packmule

Persephone

First Centurion Kosnett

Encounter at Vilahana

Consensus at Aditi

Hegemony at Dalou

Princes at Ewin

Empire at Gloran

Domain at Yaumgan

Additional Alexandria Station Stories

The Story Road

Varfelis Station

Radio Silence

Crossroads

Captain Daring

Revoked

Returned

Reborn

The Lazarus Alliance

Escape

Return

Rebellion

Revolution

Liberation

Retribution

Alliance

Shadow of the Dominion

Longshot Hypothesis

Hard Bargain

Outermost

Dominion-427

Phoenix

Princess Rualoh

RUSSIAN EMPIRE
CASPIAN SEA
ARAL SEA
KHIVA
SAMARKAND
OSH
KASHGAR
BOKHARA
CHINESE EMPIRE
PERSIA
KASHMIR
AFGHANISTAN
LAHORE

CHAPTER ONE

Looking out over the dry sands, Finn realized he'd never been to the city of Acre. Hell, he'd never been to Mandatory Palestine before this. Never made it this far east. Well, north and east. He'd been to Ethiopia too many times, but never up this far up into the old Ottoman Empire territory.

He'd landed the California Condor—his stolen Heinkel H-111 bomber/transport—on a strip outside of town, out beyond the old walls of the city that weren't there anymore. Flight up the coast had been gorgeous, with clear skies and pleasant weather.

And it helped being able to make a long flight like this on one tank of gas, instead of having to stop all the time to refill. Fellow could get used to living like this.

Assuming the Germans never figured out that he was in a stolen aircraft. According to sources Finn had asked, China had only received six of the He 111 K's—the export version of He 111 A—of the twelve that they'd ordered. Just like happened back home from time to time, the other six had fallen off the back of the truck, somewhere along the line. Or boat, as it were.

But painted up and tweaked a little during reassembly, you couldn't really tell from the outside unless you were an expert on aircraft. Inside, Hans was in the process of chipping off or painting over every swastika he could find. That man didn't appreciate what the Nazis had done to his homeland while he'd been overseas trying to make a living.

Just like everyone else in the Great Depression.

They were just hanging out right now, unpacking stuff from the rear of the plane. Him, Hans, and Emad. Zareen had started to help, but he'd barked at her maybe a little sharply and she had subsided, only going so far as to pull out a folding, cloth campaign chair and find a shady spot under a wing. Ghada, her bodyguard, was sitting next to her, the two women looking like proper passengers.

But that was fine. The boys were just the muscle around here. And employees.

Finn hadn't asked Zareen where all her money came from. Wasn't sure he really wanted to know.

She'd gotten some from the British government he knew, *sub rosa* as it were, but he also knew the woman was connected by blood to both British aristocracy and Persian nobility. He only cared because him and Hans both looked on her as something of a favored niece.

Hell, she was young enough to be his daughter, if you wanted to get technical. He'd be forty-one soon and she was twenty-two. But him and Hans had fought in the Great War. Opposite sides and all that, but after the war, a awful lot of fellows kinda knocked around a lot, looking for a next meal and a next job.

They'd both ended up flying for a sleazy Italian air company, hauling passengers on a loop from Ethiopia to Rome and back, stopping all along the way in Libya, Cyrenaica, Egypt, and the Horn. Stolen that old plane when the airline folded and nobody asked for it back.

Got hired by Zareen to...

Yeah, best not talk about that too much. His arrest warrant list was already long enough back in Chicago and the States.

Finn didn't want to think what it would add up to when you added Italian and British Colonial Authorities and their opinions on some of the things he'd done. To say nothing of the Germans.

But he turned to Zareen now as they were close to done unloading trunks and crates from the plane.

"We sure he's in Acre?" Finn asked, trying not to sound too melodramatic about it.

"We are sure that someone matching his description was seen here recently," Zareen replied, maybe a little tartly.

Maybe he deserved it, too. He'd been a little rude about her getting smelly and sweaty helping them unload the plane, after all.

"*Ve* should get him a portable radio *und* a code book, *ja?*" Hans laughed, slipping a little out of his normally pretty-good English and sounding more like the Kraut that Finn had first met.

"I have considered it, Hans," Zareen replied. "If his personal, technological sophistication were greater, one would have hoped that he would have such a device already built in, and we could have taken advantage of it."

Took Finn a second to translate that back into English, but she was like that.

"Man's a sociologist," Finn said. "Man. Robot. Whatever. Asher."

"Correct," Zareen nodded. "However, I believe that his power source would be sufficient, and the rest of the equipment would not be that large."

"Do you mean to plug a radio into his chest?" Emad spoke up now, a touch of wonder in his voice.

But he was a Bedouin. Well, as close to them as Libyan royalty raised in a palace with walls of books might be. Pretty good match for her intellectually as well as socially.

And other ways, but Finn and Hans had kept a pretty close eye on the boy. Boy. Ha. He was in his early thirties somewhere, maybe midway between the old farts and the ladies. But a gentleman.

And maybe a fellow to court Zareen. If she allowed it.

If not, he could hitch a ride back to Cyrenaica on a slow boat. Zareen made those decisions.

Finn watched her nod in reply to Emad.

"I am unsure as to his internal workings, but the man is a robot, powered by an atomic battery of some sort, if I understand," she said. "There ought to be a way to utilize that."

Finn fought not to roll his eyes. Too much like those weird scientifiction books Hans—and now Emad, too—read in his spare time to practice his English.

Sound caused his head to come round.

Finn noted an open-topped car rolling this way. Staff car kind of beast. Maybe a big Mercedes from the lines. Long hood probably hiding a twelve-cylinder powerhouse of an engine. Twin rear axles like a truck cut down.

Elegant, at least when it had been built. Kinda beat up now. But Union Jacks flew on the two front corners, so most likely an official of some sort. The friendly kind. Hopefully.

Finn nodded to Hans and Emad then stepped away from the plane to greet whoever it was. He was American. The ladies were Anglo-Persian. Hans was German. Emad was a man without a country, but in the process of taking it back from those damned fool Italians.

Finn figured he'd get along best with the stuffy Brits administering the Mandate. Hopefully they wouldn't be here all that long.

Car rolled to a stop close enough and an officer got out. World must have gone a little weird, as he was wearing heavy boots, tall socks, desert shorts, and a mostly buttoned, loose, linen shirt that might have been white.

Hard to guess his age, but Finn would have said thirty or thereabouts. Ramrod-straight spine they hammered into the kids in basic, or more likely one of those fancy military academies the Brits had.

Finn had been a mutt from Montana who enlisted in the infantry, and then managed to swing a gig as a pilot. Even survived the war, when so many others didn't. Hans had been a mechanic across the lines, so he never did shoot at anyone.

At least Finn was dressed something professional today. Zareen had sprung for new clothes for everyone, all in shades of tan that looked like uniforms without looking like uniforms.

Before the Brit could get stuffy, Finn walked over, holding out a hand to shake.

"Finnley Severijns," he said. "Flying cargo out of Cairo, but I'm hauling some important passengers sightseeing on this trip instead. Are you the fellow to talk to about ground fees and a hangar?"

Worked. Fellow got knocked off his pedestal before he could work up a good head of steam.

"Important?" he asked in a tiny voice, inaudible more than about five feet away.

Good thing Finn was close enough that the man automatically shook his hand.

"She's a Scottish noblewoman, according to what I'm told," Finn said in a quiet, conspiratorial voice, leaning in. "Got her maid with her and the rest of us are hired hands. So glad I didn't have to walk to the main building to talk to you."

"Neville Whyte, Foreign Service," the man finally found his manners. "Uhm, how long will she be staying?"

"Can't rightly guess," Finn answered. "At least overnight. Maybe a day or three. We'd like to leave the plane here, with my mechanic to watch it, while the rest of us maybe get rooms in town. On call for the mistress's needs, you know."

"Yes, of course," Whyte said, still a little lost. "This aircraft looks peculiar. Where did you acquire it?"

Well, crap. Aeronautical nerd. Probably recognized a

Heinkel, even with the things that had been done to make it look a little different.

"Are you a patriot, Whyte?" Finn let his voice grow a little hard.

Worked. The man's shoulders snapped back and his head came up.

"I am, Mister Severijns," he said.

"Well, we stole it from the Nazis when they weren't looking," Finn admitted. "The mistress secretly works for your government and will need to contact her bosses in London and let them know we're here. Can you arrange that?"

Finn figured that it would all come out eventually anyway. Especially if he got into any trouble in town and needed to call in chits.

Maybe they needed to sell the Condor and get something else, but he didn't know where he might lay hands on another medium bomber configured as a passenger liner. Maybe a Douglas DC-2 or something. Nobody else was really doing that yet, but there was another war coming.

War for the rest of them, anyway. He'd already been feuding with the Italians. Zareen was at it with a couple of French fascists. Emad had been a revolutionary in Cyrenaica.

Whyte's eyes got a little big.

"Truly?" he asked, like maybe that was the biggest thing to happen in Acre in a while.

Might be. Town was a little port city, hanging down on a peninsula sticking south into the Med. Been fought over forever.

"I'll let her explain, but just make sure to mind your manners," Finn said severely. "Woman's sharp, connected, and dangerous."

"Of course."

Finn led him over to Zareen with a crooked smile on his face.

"Lady Shirazi, this is Mister Whyte of the Foreign Service,"

Finn said. "I let him know that you'll need to contact London for updated orders and to keep things quiet while we are in town and afterwards."

Zareen rose with just a hint of sourness in her eyes, but she understood the game. They probably needed to get entirely out of the Mediterranean region for a while, especially if that Frog was still chasing her and Asher.

She stepped close and Whyte more or less half-bowed to her.

"How can I be of service, Madame?" he asked in a bright, shiny voice.

"For now, if you could haul my party into town and recommend a hotel to stay at, that gets us today," she said, rounding off her usual posh accent with some good, Highlands burr. "As Severijns said, I will need to send a message to London via cable. Can you arrange that?"

"I can, Lady Shirazi," Whyte brightened up. Looked like a man who finally had something to do this week, instead of guarding an air strip with all of three planes sitting on it at the moment, including the California Condor that had just landed.

Finn grabbed a trunk and started hauling it to the staff car. Might take two trips, but they maybe could also get enough stuffed in corners and the car boot to haul it all at once.

That got them settled in town, because Hans would sleep out here with the plane and do maintenance, as long as somebody remembered to have some food delivered from whatever hotel. The four of them could settle, get clean, and get fed.

Hopefully, there was an alien robot named Asher hiding in town for them to rescue.

CHAPTER TWO

Finn had gotten everyone settled back at the hotel. He and Emad were out exploring and making contacts, but Zareen was safe. Ghada was deadly in close combat, with knives secreted everywhere and all sorts of strange dance things she knew. Zareen had an old Broomhandle Mauser she could use to make any man understand *No*.

So the two of them were down in the souq, or whatever they called it here. Dressed like foreigners in nicer suits and hats. Blending in, at least as much as you might.

Acre was primarily a Muslim town, with a smattering of everyone else and some Zionists in the neighborhood still talking about making it a Jewish homeland. Finn wasn't exactly sure how they'd manage that, given that the locals outnumbered them pretty significantly, but if everyone could make a friendly thing out of it, wasn't his problem. Brits were trying to do something right here. History would tell if they succeeded.

Emad spoke better Arabic, but this was a British Mandate, so having a white guy along meant that the authorities wouldn't be quite so pissy about it. Wasn't like they were running guns here, or any of the other things Finn had done in his time.

And booze was legal here. *Haram*, but that was a whole different story and money was money.

Half a day gone while they'd meandered, working their way kinda clockwise, down the inner portion of the peninsula like tourists, across the tip, and then out on the sea side back up. Asking questions that didn't necessarily get answered, but that was fine as well. The man they were looking for had enemies.

Until recently, Finn supposed he was counted there, only because Zareen was after the Man With No Face along with a bunch of other folks. Before that fellow had helped Finn and Emad rescue the ladies from that French fascist, Didier Beauchêne, and joined forces with them, except that they'd gotten separated and it had been two months looking to find where the man might have gone.

When the Nazis were after you, especially for breaking into one of their prisons and rescuing a bunch of prisoners, you had to kind of lay low. Like that one time outside Iowa City, but we won't talk about that in polite company.

Mid-afternoon now. Hottest part of the day. There were a few kids that looked familiar, like maybe they'd been following Finn, but he kept things up in his jacket and harder to steal.

"Are we being successful?" Emad muttered as they exited yet another little shop, this one a tobacconist specializing in British tourists.

Crazy stuff from all over the Empire, but the Near East was kinda the hub of the civilized world. Maybe that was Suez, since stuff really entered Europe from there, instead of the huge camel trains of the old days.

"Successful is a tricky term," Finn grinned at the man.

They were about the same height, but Finn outweighed the wiry, desert warrior considerably. Both had blue eyes, though Finn's were more green.

But they'd become friends over the last while. Getting shot at a lot will do that.

"Tricky," Emad echoed sarcastically.

"If it is him, and he is here, then he needs to make sure it is us, and not that Didier punk," Finn said. "Same, we need to make sure Frenchie isn't around to cause us trouble right now."

"Tricky," Emad repeated with emphasis.

Finn grinned.

"You got it," he chuckled.

"When will we know?" Emad asked now.

"At some point, someone will have a piece of information for a few coins," Finn admitted. "We've got the money and it's a good cause. We'll find him."

"And then what?" Emad asked. "At some point, her war is larger than just Egypt and Cyrenaica."

Oh ho. That was the burr under his saddle, was it?

Finn considered his words carefully. He liked the fellow, but worked for Zareen. And considered her a niece.

"On that day, you'll have to decide if your war against Mussolini is more important than chasing after her, wherever she's headed next," Finn said seriously. "She's after something bigger. Don't know what, but she thinks it will stop the Germans, too, when they decide to get obnoxious with everybody, whenever that happens."

"There will be another Great War," Emad nodded sagely. "A greater one?"

Around them, the crowd kind of just moved like a current, with them as a rock close to one bank. Finn shifted them closer to the big, stone wall of what looked like a bank.

"Pretty sure it's impossible to not do that now," Finn told the man. "Hitler's even worse than Mussolini that way. The Japs are making noises again after what they've been doing to China, and that likely means they run headlong into the American fleet one of these days. Don't figure they can win, but that's not that same as they won't try."

"What will you do, Finn?"

"Fight," Finn said flatly. "Doing that now. Too old to put on a uniform again, probably, but I figure we're all kinda spies and agents for Zareen right now, and that won't change on that day, as long as we don't get captured or shot."

"You are an interesting man, Finn Severijns," Emad smiled.

"Remind me to tell you about the rum-running, one of these days," Finn smiled back.

He started to say more, but a figure appeared out of the crowd and beckoned him around a corner into an alley. Alleys were alleys, so he flexed his shoulders and prepared to follow, then thought better of it and just went ahead and pulled out the old Colt from his shoulder holster, holding it low against his thigh where it wasn't obvious.

Man might come at you with a knife in an alley. Not many would have a gun. Either way, white man defending himself with a pistol in that situation wasn't going to cause him to get arrested, most likely.

Finn didn't figure it said good things about human society, but Asher was correct on that tone. World was a messed up place, and the aliens were right to completely embargo all contact, at least until folks started acting better to one another.

Emad drifted back a step, just like he was flying wing. Didn't draw a gun, but Finn had seen him move quickly when he had to. And the fellow had that small cannon of a Webley under his arm.

Gentleman wanting to talk was tucked kinda back out of sight when they came around the corner. Not hiding but not standing in the open. He flinched a little at the visible firepower, but nodded with lips pressed together.

A hand was held out silently, and Finn put a one pound note into it, causing the man to look up in surprise.

"Hopefully, what you've got is worth that, right?" he asked in Arabic.

Fellow sputtered a little, and then gave Finn an address, deep in the heart of the slums around here, small as they might be.

"It is dangerous for one such as you," he nodded, indicating white as opposed to Arabic, but Finn just grinned and put the pistol away.

"Really just want to talk to the man," Finn said. "Assuming it's him. Anybody else wanting to cause trouble... Well, they'll get more than they bargained for, won't they?"

The man's eyes got huge, but he tucked the bill away and scampered off down the alley without looking back.

Finn nodded and hoped he'd bluffed the man correctly.

"Now what?" Emad asked.

"Now we go see a man about a horse," Finn replied.

CHAPTER THREE

Asher sat and contemplated the afternoon sun as it started to fade outside. He was in his preferred type of business, a coffee shop that would let him rent a table in a quiet corner for a large chunk of the day but not require him to actually drink anything while he was here.

It was sufficient to allow the humans around him to think that he wanted the company but did not wish to subject anyone to a ruined face. He wore a steel mask, after all, painted over with enamel to look close enough to flesh tone.

In Cairo, he had been just one of a number of such men injured in a previous military event, generally the so-called Great War, all of whom hid their faces. If there were fewer here, it was still a useful cover.

He had originally been delivered to Earth with an outer shell that would be indistinguishable from human to the medical science of the day, X-rays notwithstanding. It had been burned off in the crash that had destroyed his ship and killed all his friends, leaving a forlorn mechanoid stranded on an alien planet and attempting to survive.

Autonomous Simulated Human Exploration Robot, Mark

Eight. In English, which was a predominant language in much of this region, it made a useful enough acronym.

Asher.

He had hidden in Cairo for a generation before the outside world intruded. Then he had joined with Zareen Shirazi and her comrades for a time, before being separated and going into hiding again.

Now rumor suggested that they had finally managed to find his trail, without bringing that fascist chap along with them.

Didier Beauchêne and his assassin Bertrand would be a problem, but Asher was programmatically prohibited from harming a human. Thus he had hidden then, and remained hidden now, although nothing in his code required him to stop Finn Severijns, Hans Fertig, or Emad al-Sadri from hurting the others.

And probably making Earth a better place, but he would never tell them that.

He had been put here to study humans originally. The Durren were fascinated and appalled in equal amounts by the species, but did not understand them at all. Asher had a much better grasp now, but they would no doubt dismantle his chassis and end his consciousness when they finally realized that he had been snuck in here against all regulations. Hopefully, they would save his datacore first.

Or he would find a deep ocean and walk out there when his powercells finally began to fade, just so no humans would ever be able to understand what he really was under these robes.

Hopefully, that would not have to happen today. Asher was not sure, as rumors had swirled.

A man entered the shop and looked around quickly before moving this direction. Asher knew the fellow by reputation, but he had not had the luxury of getting to know all the information brokers in Acre well. But in Cairo, he had been a fixture for twenty years when he left.

The man was a local. A Muslim who seemed to make most

of his money in the smuggling business, although Asher had not pressed. Illegal transport of unlicensed goods seemed to be a time-honored tradition in many human cultures, a thing to be nodded at and generally ignored for certain bribes.

But Asher already knew that humans were insane by galactic standards.

The man sat and waved for the keeper to bring him some coffee. The place was known for a particularly Turkish style of coffee. Asher did not have taste buds anymore to judge, but the locals apparently liked it thick and heavy.

"Two men come, seeking you, I think, my friend," the man said after the coffee was delivered and they were alone again. "Both tall. One looked American, the other Arab, but not a local. Egyptian, perhaps."

"Asking for the Man With No Face?" Asher asked.

"Not in absolute terms, no," the man said. "The American is satisfied to ask and keep walking, as if planting seeds rather than hunting. They have so far walked halfway around the waterfront, and seem to be content to continue."

Asher nodded. It sounded like Finn and Emad. Hans would have remained with the aircraft. Zareen Shirazi would be trapped by both her lineages if she tried to insert herself into the local culture, and thus thwarted, but likely she and Ghada were nearby. Perhaps at one of two nice hotels that catered to the British.

"Did they arrive by aircraft?" Asher asked.

The man flinched and his eyes fell.

"Perhaps, but the aircraft, according to others, might be a German model," he said. "A bomber, although it is painted in civilian colors. Germans are not well-liked in this region."

"It was a German plane," Asher assured the man. "Friends in Cairo stole it and put it to use fighting the Nazis. Tell me, what would the local population think if the Germans and the British went to war again?"

"Some would support each side," came the answer. "The

British are overlords that many wish to kick out so we can be free, but the Germans seek to extend their Reich and thus would just be different masters, perhaps with a heavier touch. The British support the Zionists, so there is much fervor against both groups in Jerusalem, but Acre is a trading port, and war is bad for business."

Asher suspected as much. Zareen seemed to be the rule, rather than the exception, except that she was quietly working to liberate her homeland from all outsiders. She and Beauchêne each hoped to find or create superweapons, with his help or in spite of it. Alien technology they could use in their desired war. Shirazi would use it to defend Persia from all outsiders. Beauchêne would overthrow the French Republic and join forces with German and Italian fascists to plunge the world into conflagration.

And humans were on the verge of industrial technologies that would perhaps end them as a species if they were not careful.

Asher nodded at the news.

"When I was in Cairo, there was a man," he began, spinning off a story about one of the many smugglers that worked Suez and the Red Sea to effectively thwart British control.

Asher heard many things. His hearing apparatus was powerful enough that he could dial up the gain and follow every conversation in the coffee shop separately at the same time. Even whispers were shouts to his ears.

He had made a living as an information broker then. He was well on his way to doing the same here. It involved a complicated calculus of trading tidbits and favors. Right now, he did not have sufficient credit or credibility, so he gave greater value than he generally received, but that would change with time.

Or not. If Zareen Shirazi had finally located him, perhaps it was time to rejoin her mission to stop the fascists from conquering the species. Asher wasn't sure what a machine such as him could do, but she seemed confident.

That mattered to him, he found.

After a time, his guest finished his coffee and Asher finished his story. The man rose and departed, perhaps with a jauntier stride than he had entered with. But information and value had been exchanged.

The Durren didn't grasp the finer points of capitalism. His knowledge alone would greatly expand their learning, if he was ever allowed to go home.

He checked the angle of the sunlight out the window and noted that the British would probably be rushing for High Tea about now. And a message would be making its way to Finn and Emad, if it was them.

Asher noted the two entrances to the coffee shop, facing either side of the corner of the block, as well as the one to the kitchen and rear, where it would empty onto a small alleyway that served several other businesses.

No human understood how quickly this chassis could move if pressed. He generally wished to appear human in all things, down to the robes, boots, gloves, hood, and mask. But he was still an exploration robot, meant to survive great perils unharmed.

Hopefully, he would.

CHAPTER FOUR

Didier sat in the chair and ground his teeth, all the while maintaining a calm exterior as the woman lectured him in an angry, almost shrill voice. She was dressed as a civilian, but he knew her and her companion to be Nazi officials. *Schutzstaffel.* The dreaded *SS* itself. The room was barely large enough for all the egos packed in here.

"Now that we have detailed all your failures, Beauchêne, do you have any questions?" she demanded.

Didier would have gladly had Bertrand kill the woman, but he needed her, much as it galled him. The French fascists he worked with had proven to be as unreliable as any might expect, caught up in their silly, Gallic superiority when Didier knew that the Germans were far more than just a match.

"No, Fraulein Reiher," he said, biting off each syllable so his anger did not bleed out. "Shirazi has accumulated unexpected resources since she arrived in Cairo. Plus, we suspect that she did indeed find something out in the desert, but the team I sent to explore has disappeared entirely. It was as if the sands swallowed them whole."

"So you turned to us," she completed the thought for him, scowling and haughty.

Didier preferred the French ideal of beauty, but he was stuck with the woman that his Nazi party contacts had assigned when it became clear what had happened to that prison in Cyrenaica. Important people in Germany were taking notice of things now, for good or ill.

Fraulein Zofija Reiher. A tall, busty, blond, *Übermenschen* woman, built with muscles like a Bavarian peasant, except that he knew her to have competed against men in modern pentathlons.

She was everything the French knew better than to desire, except perhaps the tall part. He preferred a skinny waif of a woman with brown hair and green eyes. A model, perhaps, rather than an *athlete*.

But Shirazi had reduced him to a form of beggarage, so he had to take what came with it.

"I came to you," he agreed sourly.

Reiher smiled down at him and them moved to stand off to one side, apparently making way for her companion to berate Didier now.

At least Dr. Konrad Schwarzenberg was a scientist. A cruel man Didier had encountered at fascist gatherings over the last decade or two, but one given over to science, rather than that silly metaphysical mumbo-jumbo that other parts of the Nazi party had decided represented the future.

As if the Holy Grail or the Ark of the Covenant would be magically discovered today and then turn their power to the Nazi cause.

He refrained from rolling his eyes, unsure if Reiher was a *True Believer* like some.

"So, Didier, we have heard your stories," Konrad said as he moved from the wall and took a chair across the small table.

The apartment was crowded, even with just the three of them, but Bertrand had been instructed to remain outside nearby as a guard. And to probably keep the man from reacting to the Germans and their abuse. At least he had mostly recovered from Severijns shooting him in the back during their last fiasco.

Didier finally gave up and reached into his jacket for his cigarettes. The nicotine would calm his nerves right now and having something in his mouth would keep him from blurting things out.

Hopefully.

Konrad pulled a pack of Turkish cigarillos and lit one at the same time, bringing something of a respite to the angry heat contained in the room.

Fraulein Reiher moved to the window and opened it, kipping one impossibly long leg up and resting her muscular bottom on the sill, presumably to breathe the cleaner air outside.

Seriously, what man found such a woman attractive?

But he smoked and that helped.

Konrad focused cold, blue eyes on him, as if weighing his soul.

"You still believe that the Man With No Face is an alien?" Konrad asked. "A little green man from Mars?"

"Someplace," Didier agreed vaguely. "All the clues suggest it and I have found nothing to dispute it. However, without actually capturing the man himself, I cannot know."

"And you think he will lead you to his spaceship?" Reiher scoffed from the window, but Konrad's face was more serious.

"I think something originally happened in the desert in 1916," Didier replied, finding calmness now. "She went there and returned to immediately locate him. A French exploration vanished a month ago. By now, I presume that they were killed. We need to locate the Man With No Face and capture him. It is as simple as that."

"Lucky for you, then, that Air Force Command has decided to take a greater interest," Konrad smiled. "Watchers have been instructed to locate that aircraft and report. It is stolen property, after all, so even the British will have to assist us, once she is located. Then we will find out what she knows."

Didier took a long drag on his cigarette in order to not curse aloud. The Germans had been his last resort at this point, with much of his money stolen at some point and the woman vanished. Back home, the French government was making noises about arresting him again, so his connections were wary of helping him, even with all the money he had available in Swiss banks and other places.

But he would have to share anything he discovered with the Germans. That much was obvious. On the other hand, if that helped them conquer the world, Didier had no doubts that they would remember the people who helped.

Assuming the Fraulein wasn't an assassin here to seduce all of his secrets away from him before killing him. Except that they would have been better served with a more attractive woman on that front.

A knock at the door interrupted. Reiher drew a Luger pistol from her coat and moved off to one side. Konrad did the same.

Didier made a mental note to remind them to carry less obvious firearms in the future, as Lugers just screamed *Nazi!* to most people.

He rose and drew his little semi-automatic .25 pocket pistol. The one that he had improved significantly.

"Who's there?" he called through the door.

"Bertrand," the assassin's voice hissed back, just barely audible. "And guest."

Guest?

Didier opened the door and pulled it just enough to peek.

Of course the man was in full German military uniform. Did these people have no concept of keeping a low profile? Didier could only imagine the number of British spies that had probably followed the fool to his doorstep.

Obviously, he would need to leave Cairo immediately. Perhaps he could spread a rumor of being hunted by the

Germans rather than turning to them for help, just to salvage his reputation.

"In quickly, you fools," he snapped, pulling the door open and gesturing both in.

The messenger carried a bag. He extracted an envelope now as he clicked his heels together. Didier read his own name on the side and studied the man and envelope.

Luftwaffe, from the uniform, so not a spy. Just a soldier.

I am surrounded by buffoons. Dangerous ones, to be sure, but amateurs at this business.

Didier took it and ripped it open quickly, studying the message. It was a cable.

AIRCRAFT LOCATED. ACRE IN BRITISH PALESTINE. SHIRAZI AND OTHERS.

The original message was sent three days ago.

THREE DAYS?!? Had those fools routed it through Berlin first?

Didier caught his breath short of an explosion of profanities. In pursuing Shirazi, more than once the difference of three hours had been sufficient for her to escape him. At Lisbon, it had gotten her all the way to Cairo, and only a fast aircraft when she had taken a ship across the water had allowed him to keep even that close.

He folded the letter and handed it to Konrad.

Didier really wanted to pull out a few Francs for the Luftwaffe man, as if he was a bell boy, but decided that the others might read that for the insult he intended and take offense.

"Good, you may go," he told the man instead, nodding to Bertrand to get him out of the room and out of their lives while there might still be a chance to salvage things.

Alone again, the three of them, he studied his co-conspirators closely.

Fraulein Reiher scowled, but he expected no less of the woman. Konrad smiled.

"On to Acre, it seems?" he asked lightly.

"As a start." Didier returned Reiher's scowl in spades. "By now I am certain they have moved on again, so we will be chasing them to wherever she goes next."

"Already, *Herr* Doctor?" Reiher asked.

"Three days," he sneered at her. "And they know we are after them. That is why it has been so difficult to locate them before now."

"Then we should not waste any more time," she smiled serenely. "I wish to make the acquaintance of the woman who had bested you up until now."

Didier kept his mouth a smile for now. Perhaps he should introduce this woman to the American. Severijns.

Let them destroy each other.

CHAPTER FIVE

Finn studied the place from across the street and down a half block or so, just listening to the flow of people and traffic. He'd learned the trick in Kansas City and Chicago back in the Twenties.

When the police were hanging around, the noise got different. Housewives would talk sharper or not at all, rather than just calling the usual patter and snide commentary at each other as the day progressed. Layabouts would suddenly find more interesting places to be, afraid that they might be rousted or arrested if the cops were nearby.

Even in Arabic, half a world away, the patterns didn't change. Dress everyone here Western style in pants and shirts and floppy hats. Change the calls to Polish or Yiddish or Italian and you'd think you were back home. The only big cue was the smell. Back home, it would be pork and tomatoes warring with each other. Here, it was more couscous and beef in a variety of weird spices he'd tried but never really gotten his head around.

But there weren't any cops nearby. That was really the big key right now. He could deal with Italians or maybe Germans that had finally tracked them down, but he was more concerned about British folks asking why a white man with a shady past was down here in these neighborhoods.

Didn't need to get hauled in as a potential smuggler. Too many people might start asking questions with answers that got a mite complicated.

He turned to Emad and watched the other man. Emad didn't seem to sense any trouble either, but he was more accustomed to royal palaces and deep desert than small towns like this. Emad smiled and nodded back.

Finn hunched his shoulders once and touched his cap. Zareen had insisted that he dress a little better today, so he had a Fedora for the sun, but he forgot about it most of the time. Made him look respectable, he supposed, which might be a problem over the long term, but today he was more a tourist than anything.

You'll believe that, right?

The crowd seemed to part as they moved, little fishies slipping around them without touching, but he and Emad were well-dressed foreigners, and he could only imagine that there were two worlds around here. *With* and *without* money, and all the issues that went along with it.

Coffee shop got clearer as he got closer. Turkish, though filtered down the whole Levant coast by local tastes, so dark and rich, the thick stuff, but sweeter around here. Might even be drinkable, but he'd withhold judgment.

Finn wasn't even sure he'd actually drink any. Not in a strange place that might not be above a Mickey Finn.

Local kids hanging around started to beg, but he scowled and they subsided quick enough, so Finn entered the joint.

Arabic coffee shop, right out of a movie set, with rickety tables and exotic characters. Finn didn't know if they got it right back in Hollywood or if these folks watched those movies and decorated accordingly, but he felt like he'd been here before. Fat guy hovering and suddenly nervous about well-dressed strangers intruding in what felt like a neighborhood joint, so Finn smiled at him.

"Coffee for me and my friend," he said amiably in Arabic, looking around.

About half the tables were in use, so he moved to an empty one and sat, but not until he noted a familiar-looking enameled-steel face over in a corner with a good view and several doors nearby.

Emad started to speak, but Finn glared at him. They ended up at a table close, but not that close.

"I presume we're scouting for ambushes," Emad murmured as the owner tapped the big, brass samovar and bought two steaming cups over.

Finn nodded. It was close enough, anyway. Emad had never run rum into Chicago.

They sat and sipped their coffee as the volume came back up closer to normal. Finn didn't figure it would return to what it had been before, until about ten minutes after he left, but that was fine.

He was watching back over his shoulder, at least metaphorically.

Emad was, too, so nobody was sneaking up on them in here.

A few minutes passed. He and Emad chatted quietly and amiably while sipping the fresh tar, trying to put the locals at ease. Wasn't going to work, but he could at least not make it any worse.

Nobody came storming in. Not British officials stomping up to ask what the hell he thought he was doing, either.

A figure eventually rose in the corner and stepped close, wearing the sorts of flowing robes folks wore in the open desert to keep bugs and heat off you. The face was incapable of smiling, but the eye slits seemed to convey it anyway.

"Please, join us," Finn said loud enough for the locals to hear.

Maybe it would calm things.

Asher took a chair and settled.

"I had wondered how long it might take for you to catch up," Asher said quietly, leaning forward now to put metal elbows covered in sleeves on the table. "But I have been using my time to good value."

"Well, you are an incredibly difficult man to locate, my friend," Finn said. "And we had to stay out of sight as well after that rude stunt we pulled in Libya, so that made it harder to search."

"Indeed. It is enough that you have gotten here at last," Asher said. "And according to my contacts, it is all of you, yes?"

"Yup," Finn smiled. "Emad and I are blending in, as much as we can. Hans is back with the California Condor. The ladies are across from the embassy at the hotel."

"Excellent," Asher said. "I will need to talk to Zareen, and possibly derail her current plans, such as they might be."

"Oh?" Emad leaned forward now, setting his coffee down.

Finn nodded. This might be that point where the man had to fork the road and pick his path.

Or his destiny. You never knew. Certainly, Finn could have gone back to Montana in '19 and taken up the life of a countryman.

Man, that would've been boring as all get out.

"I have found a map, and translated it," Asher announced with the sorts of gravity the guy on the World Service used at night.

"And?" Finn prompted, just like a straight guy in any Vaudeville routine.

"And it might be Durren," Asher said.

Aw, hell.

CHAPTER SIX

Zareen listened as Asher completed his tale. They were all in her hotel room, save for Hans, back at the airstrip, but he preferred that level of solitude so she would not begrudge the man. She would send a car out to bring him into town for dinner, and they would perhaps only stay tonight.

She looked down at the map that Asher had brought with him. Hand-drawn on a stiff parchment intended to be rolled back into its scroll tube for storage.

The terrain was mountainous in nature, but none of the locations were places she was familiar with. The big clue was that it was written in what Asher had called a variant of an ancient Indic script.

"How ancient?" she asked, looking up again across the table at her friend.

It was just the two of them seated in this hotel suite, even though there was space and chairs. Ghada hovered nearby. Finn actually sat on the back of the couch in her sitting area. Emad was leaned against a wall, looking nervous.

Asher cleared his throat, which was an impressive acoustic feat, considering that he didn't have a throat. But it served the same purpose of clarifying the conversation.

"According to legend, the Tibetan script was created in the mid-Seventh Century AD after a minister of the government named Thonmi Sambhota was sent to India," Asher explained. "He returned with a written language and instituted it, if the stories I have encountered in my research are correct."

"Tibet?" she asked, somewhat nervous.

Her expertise had been largely European and Persian in scope, ranging as far east as perhaps Samarkand on the Silk Road. Beyond that was much more unknown to Zareen, as was its history.

"So you believe that this map originates on the Himalayan Plateau?" Zareen confirmed.

"And that it was subsequently brought here via either a merchant or perhaps one of the military incursions into the area, such as when the British invaded in 1904 to block the Russians from moving south in their so-called Great Game," Asher agreed.

"So you would have us seeking Shambala?" she followed up, smiling a little that the ancient myths and legends might yield a kernel of truth.

"I cannot tell you if Mr. Hilton had anything other than wild stories upon which to base his book, Zareen," Asher said, his voice turning serious now. "But I recognize certain symbols and words on this map that no other person on this planet should."

"Because they are not a lost hieroglyph, but written Durren?"

She felt her stomach go cold at the thought. How long had those aliens been studying Earth? Until quite recently, the species was technologically primitive, after all, only achieving mass industry in the last one hundred and fifty years or so.

"Indeed," Asher agreed.

Zareen looked up and caught Finn's eye, unwilling to try to convince Emad yet. That would be another mountain to climb.

"Will your aircraft handle such a flight?" she asked, trying to sound innocent.

The California Condor belonged to Finn. Their arrangement was that she hired him and Hans, and the plane, even though they had all become much closer than mere employees.

He stirred now, stepping forward.

"Asher, what are the old Silk Road towns we might stop at to get fuel, with a working range of about twenty-two hundred kilometers?" he asked their new tour guide.

"From here, perhaps Tehran, then Samarkand, then Kashgar," Asher said. "That would put you at the western edge of a great desert basin, tracing the old road backwards, although you would head south and west from there, according to this map."

Finn grunted and nodded to her, apparently satisfied that he could do such a thing. The German bomber was such an improvement over his old Ford Trimotor, after all. A modern medium bomber comfortable for six and their luggage, when it was just four plus the two pilots.

"Kashgar," Zareen said. "The old gates to China."

"The same," Asher agreed.

"Why, Asher?" she turned her attention to the alien robot. "After so long hiding from humanity, why have you decided to take an active role? This might, after all, blow your cover."

"The Durren seek to understand humanity, Zareen," he said.

Then he surprised her by reaching up and removing his mask to reveal the steel-like face underneath, the raw metal and shell that had been covered once by pseudo-flesh so that he could walk among them as a social geographer.

"I had to be smuggled in secretly, because my mission was illegal under Durren code, and unethical as well," Asher continued. "They do not believe that human civilization will survive industrial war, but that you will destroy yourselves and perhaps end all things, once you begin understanding what powers can be unlocked by mastering the atom."

"Bombs?" Emad asked in a quiet voice.

"City-killers," Asher turned that way. "County-killers. Perhaps nation-killers, if you were to use several, which would induce retaliation once everyone was so armed, thereby spreading the devastation. Your kind are not that far removed from discovering bronze, my friend. It would not take much to return you there."

"And you wish to help," Zareen stated, rather than asking.

"The fascists will create an unstable structure if they win." He turned back to her now. "I am not a scientist, but I am a specialist in human cultures. Democracy has flaws, but is a better model than the Italians or Nazis would institute, given the chance. If I can help you stop them, then perhaps I help humanity thread its way through the eye of the needle to a more socially advanced place beyond. I do not know what you would find there, but it might help."

Zareen nodded. Drew a breath and looked at Finn and Emad. Asher was committed. Ghada was, as well.

"I believe that we should explore what this map suggests," she said carefully. "Perhaps it might help defeat the Italians sooner, and stop the Germans before they decide to take over the world. I would like your help."

Emad's face was pain, but in Acre he was already farther from home than he had ever been in his life. She knew that. She also knew that it might be too much to ask him to accompany her around the world. That would sadden her, but she would continue on.

He wouldn't be the first man to decide that her adventures were more than he wished to participate in, but only Ghada knew those truths.

Finn seemed to understand, because he stood up now and nodded to her.

"Not like we're that far away," he said. "Condor can get us back here just as fast as we get there when we're done," he said, hedging things somewhat by turning to include Emad as he spoke.

Emad paused and considered.

"It will help the war effort," Zareen said.

"I understand that," Emad said. "And my cousin supports me in that. I will need to send him a message. Not so they can find me, but so they know how long I expect to be gone. At least a month, I presume, but we can always cable more news. As Finn suggested, the world is much smaller than it used to be."

Zareen felt a load come off her shoulders as Emad smiled crookedly at her. Finn as well.

"Let us send a car for Hans, then," she said, looking at everyone. "We need to have a happy dinner tonight, and then pack everything we might need to leave tomorrow."

CHAPTER SEVEN

Didier would have liked to remain an independent operative, but he might never be free of the Germans again. He had wondered idly over dinner if he should consider arranging for an accident to befall the rest of them at some point, just so he could escape Fraulein Reiher and her glowing, sapphire eyes. Bertrand would not mind, as he had been relegated to almost a bit part by the Germans.

The woman was a sexual predator. Everyone in the restaurant recognized that, but none could say who her prey would be. He had held off her suggestions in Cairo and again here in Acre, but worried that at some point she would no longer take no for an answer.

Perhaps a reputation for impotence would be a lesser evil? Even for a Frenchman? Certainly he didn't think he would be faking such a condition if that woman suddenly appeared on his doorstep with *demands*.

And Konrad was no help, remaining a dry, dour man most of the time. Didier wondered if she had already used and discarded the fool like the empty husks on a spider's web.

At least the restaurant was adequate. English, but the chef had some aspirations to cuisine, so there were French options available, as long as he didn't look too closely at how his meal had arrived where it had.

The manager had seated them away from the regular guests somewhat, on a platform Didier supposed was intended to make people remotely visible, if you wanted to show yourself off. Or be shown off.

Didier did not appreciate being a show pony today, but Reiher was in her element. Proper attire had required she wear a dress tonight instead of dressing as a man or a horsewoman. She did not fool anyone by suggesting demureness, but at least she had to pretend, if only for a few hours.

He and Konrad were in suits, brown in his case and gray in Konrad's, as befitted gentlemen scholars at dinner.

Their remoteness from the rest of the room also meant that they could indulge in conversation, as long as they remained quiet. At some point, there might even be music, but it was early and Didier had no intention of being subjected to English entertainment if he wanted his digestion to succeed.

"How long until your spies determine where they went?" Didier asked sharply, focusing on Konrad rather than dealing with the depth of cleavage Reiher was prominently displaying this evening.

Didier had images of the infamous Venus Flytrap plant whenever he looked at the woman.

Konrad shrugged.

"The message has gone out to all stations to be watchful for that aircraft," he replied simply. "We know they took off from Acre headed east, but whether they circled around later is unknown. The Heinkel H-111 has an exceptional range, after all, especially if one is merely traveling rather than dropping bombs on Spanish Socialists."

Didier didn't know if the man had been part of the Condor Legion in Spain, but he wouldn't have been surprised. Those men were all *mercenaries*, according to the public news. German mercenaries in uniforms, but still.

Didier wanted to say more, but movement by the door caught his eye.

Another fool in German uniform, walking right in on them at dinner in front of God and everyone else.

*Have you people **no** understanding of subtlety or tradecraft? Could it not have waited another hour?*

Worse, the man walked right up to Reiher and handed her an envelope, bowed, and silently departed.

Didier felt every eye in the club on him right now, measuring him as a Nazi spy, most likely.

The British were fussy, but had remained politically neutral for now. And he could claim to be merely a guest, at least until someone tracked all of them to Cairo and uncovered his history.

Then his reputation would be shot. How bad did he want this help to track Shirazi and kill her?

Reiher opened the missive and read it quickly before handing it to Konrad.

"Well this is most interesting," he said, sharing a smile with the woman as he passed the note to Didier.

It was a copy of a cable, apparently sent by someone in Shirazi's group to Cairo to be forwarded to Idris of Cyrenaica, the pretender to the Libyan throne. Bribes in Acre had apparently been sufficient to jar information out of the telegraph office.

"Kashgar?" Didier asked aloud, utterly surprised.

Konrad shrugged at him.

Didier wondered if the Persian woman had fallen for all the silly clap-trap of the Shambala legends that had grown up around that fantastical book. Everyone knew that the Tibetans were primitives. Hitler and his paranormalists had infiltrated all manner of agents into the region looking for metaphysical power they thought the Orientals must be hiding with all their other things.

He read the note again.

Departing Acre yesterday, just hours before Didier had

gotten here, thence to Tehran. From there to Samarkand on the old central Silk Road, and eventually Kashgar, out on the edge of the Chinese desert.

Bizarrely, no farther, which suggested that they were not headed to China from there, but remaining in the vicinity of Tibet, as you could fly up onto the plateau from there.

Shambala indeed.

"Why would she be going there, Beauchêne?" Reiher asked now.

It was Didier's turn to shrug.

"The woman is seeking the same thing I am, Fraulein," he replied. "Proof of scientific, otherworldly contact, but not angels or demons."

"Aliens," she said simply.

"Who is to say that Wells or Verne were right or wrong in their ramblings?" he countered her grimace. "Everyone is currently trying to figure out how to actually get into space, from just discovering heavier-than-air flight less than four decades ago. If other worlds exist and are more sophisticated than we are, one would expect them to visit, no?"

"And the Man With No Face?" Konrad asked.

"Rumors suggest that he is an alien, Dr. Schwarzenberg," Didier reminded him. "Certainly he seems to be able to speak and read any language put before him. And there was even a rumor of a mugger who struck him with a stick to no effect."

"Is he dangerous?" Reiher's eyes gleamed.

Didier wondered if that was the sort of thing that aroused the woman. He suppressed a disgusted shudder. Germans were insane. The Nazis had just reveled in it and used such a thing.

"I cannot know until we locate him, Fraulein," Didier said. "And apparently that trail will perhaps lead us across the top of the world in order to answer that. Can we catch him?"

"We can try," Konrad said. "They have a day and a half lead on us now, but nothing in their message suggests that they are in a great hurry, so perhaps we can give chase."

"What if it is all a sham?" Reiher asked. "A ploy to get us away from Egypt or Libya while they attack another target like they did that prison in Bengasi?"

"Unlikely," Konrad said. "If for no other reason than news of the aircraft has gone out over all channels and people will be looking for it. I would think that they would only have two choices at this point, to depart the region, or sell the aircraft and acquire a new one."

"So we are going to Tibet?" Didier confirmed.

"So it would seem, Dr. Beauchêne."

He kept his grumbles to himself. At least there nobody would know his soon-to-be-destroyed reputation as a French patriot.

At least until after these two were removed from the game.

CHAPTER EIGHT

Finn figured that this trip was just going to be plumb full of "never done that before" moments. And places he'd only ever studied on a map because he was bored and flew places, so he might need to know where he was going if somebody hired him to do something crazy.

Crazier, maybe.

The California Condor had soared regally over the realms of Jordan, Iraq, and now he was on the far side of Persia. He'd even asked Zareen if she wanted to make a side stop to visit family, however briefly, but had gotten the most monumental scowl in response, so he'd dropped it entirely and concentrated on flying and keeping Hans from telling dirty jokes. Too many dirty jokes.

Helped that most of the ones he knew were in German and didn't translate worth a damn into English or Arabic.

So Tehran was behind them. Herat had been an option, if he wanted to swing south through British India, but the hump up would be a pain, so it was easier to float through Central Asia. Fewer mountain ranges to deal with, if nothing else, although endless desert and scrub could bore any man to sleep.

Map said he could kind of slip across the edge of a long mountain range past Osh and then cut over, but Finn had no idea what the political situation would be like. The Russians had bailed on the Great War in '17 and had a revolution or six. Commies were in charge now, and didn't like outsiders. Couldn't say he really blamed them, considering all the things the Allies and the Whites had done to try to keep the Reds out of power in the early '20s.

Lots of old Russian nobility living or maybe hiding in Paris and the States these days as a result. Hopefully, they'd look at him as just a tourist, especially if he was flying onward to Kashgar and maybe told folks he was eventually headed someplace like Chunking.

Misdirection didn't sound all that bad, since a lot of Central Asia was a little rough these days, at least on a map.

"I need a nap," Hans announced.

Finn wasn't surprised. You could almost set your watch by it, but the big Kraut was a predicable sort. And could sleep through anything while they were flying.

Pretty quick Finn was alone, but not for long. The interior hatch opened again and then closed. Didn't change the noise much, but altered the tone some.

He was surprise when Zareen sat down and picked up the headphones and mic, putting them on and looking over at him. Finn had left his down around his neck, since Hans was loud enough, but he pulled them up now.

But she didn't talk. Just sat there and maybe stewed a little, from the intense concentration on her face.

Finn glanced back, but the hatch was closed. This was about as private as it got until they landed in Samarkand this evening.

"I have a question," she finally said, about the time he wondered if she'd changed her mind.

Finn nodded for her to proceed.

"How far can we go before Emad recoils, do you suppose?" she asked.

Finn felt his head snap around pretty hard. Good thing his hands were on a different channel and didn't jerk the plane over onto a wing when he did that.

Her smile was a little brittle, but then he realized what she was asking.

"Hans and I are in for the duration, I'm guessing," Finn said. "The alternative is that stupid hat and uniform the Italians made us wear. Emad now..."

He drifted off and thought about it.

From that first ambush out in the middle of nowhere, the man had turned into a pretty good friend. Hadn't gotten all that close to Zareen in a physical sense, not that anybody would have minded, as long as he behaved, but the act of not doing anything maybe suggested how serious both of them looked at it.

Favorite uncle time?

"You're better off talking to him directly at some point, ya know," Finn continued. "Right now, he's part of the team, and we're committed to doing a thing. As long as it hurts the Italians somehow, I figure he's there. How soon do you figure to start deviating from that radio beacon?"

Took her a couple of moments to get that, but she wasn't a flyer. Just an adventurer.

"This might be pushing those limits," she said.

"Better that you did it up front, then," Finn replied. "Get him used to globe-trotting, as it were. We know you're all about finding, recovering, or discovering some new technological wonder to make weapons with. It'll help the Brits and the friendlies, at least for now."

It was her time to snap around in surprise, but Finn just grinned. Wasn't like she'd been too secretive about things. And a man has to be able to read the weather to fly strange places.

They couldn't stop in Tehran or anywhere in Persia to say hello, but that was because folks would wonder about Emad al-Sadri and whether he was a suitor. Or a suitable one, anyway.

Finn knew the man was, but he also understood that some folks get a little full of themselves from time to time and don't necessarily see the big picture. Probably they'd have to slip up to Scotland at some point as well, just to have a chat with that grandmother and maybe Zareen's retired father.

Because when this youngster was done whooping the Italians into shape, and maybe the Germans, Finn figured Great Britain and the Soviet Union were probably next on her list.

He could read a map and see who threatened Persia's borders.

"And you'll still support me?" Zareen asked, a touch of wonder in her voice.

Finn grinned.

"If the Canadians or Mexicans decided to get fresh, I'd be looking to kick them in the teeth," he replied. "John Pershing notwithstanding, or any of the stupid crap the marines have gotten up to in Central America. It's your home. One of them, anyway. We'll have to stomp the Italians like cockroaches first, and I'm already in favor of doing that after the way their government has treated me and Emad."

"Then you will enjoy Samarkand," she smiled at him. "It is still full of the sorts of shifty characters and revolutionary fervor that Cairo had."

Finn nodded. Lots of that going around these days, but he figured that was part of what was going to drive the next big war. The world was changing and a lot of folks didn't like the status quo. Too many of them were probably going to resort to guns to try to change it.

And he might help, depending.

She rose suddenly, hanging the headphones from the back of the seat.

Surprised the absolute hell out of him when she leaned over

and planted a kiss on the top of his head like a mom with a kid. But he was an uncle. And maybe he'd given her what she needed to think about before they got to the top of the world and looked around.

She'd saved him from wherever he'd been drifting off to. Maybe it was time to return the favor.

CHAPTER NINE

Finn studied the town from the airstrip where he'd put the California Condor down. It had been great originally. Sacked more than once. Abandoned and rebuilt, but it was still fabled Samarkand, one of the jewels on the silk road that had historically bound the world together.

You'd be hard pressed to see all that now, but the revolutions had moved people around. Used to be the regional capital, according to a book he'd bought in Tehran from one of the merchants when they spent the night. Tashkent had supplanted it a few years ago. Those two and Bukhara were still three pearls on a strand.

Finn'd stayed up all night reading about the region, just so he was prepared. Didn't figure he'd be able to talk to anyone, as they mostly spoke Tajik, but the book said they were able to understand the Persian Zareen spoke, as long as you didn't call it a bastardized dialect.

Them might be fightin' words around here.

A truck was approaching. Battered flatbed with one man in the cab.

Finn was dressed in his flying gear, comfortable with a jacket over his shoulder holster. Emad was dressed western style, as were both of the women, just to look like rich tourist foreigners. Hans never changed out of his regular pants and shirt, but that might be why he preferred to stay with the plane more of the time. None of that cloak and dagger stuff and he never had to wear a pretty hat.

Finn stepped forward, gesturing Zareen close.

Driver parked and got out. Average-looking guy. Maybe forty. Started speaking and Finn didn't follow any of it. Big surprise there.

Zareen went right at him, though, and it was fun watching the man's eyes get big as he realized why the pretty woman was speaking. She even managed to sound BBC Evening Service in her accent, poshest London in spite of Persian.

Fellow near fell over himself bowing and scraping pretty quick.

"I believe we have established a basis for a relationship." She turned to him and spoke in haughty English now.

Finn kept his face serious. Other fellow was too far away to see the smile in his eyes.

"So we'll need a fuel truck for Hans, as well as water and maybe some fresh food," Finn nodded. "Then I presume five of us in town for the night?"

The sun wasn't low, but there was nowhere he wanted to try to fly to in the dark. Not this far from Cairo or Rome. Condor could get them where they needed to go by mid-day tomorrow, if they got a reasonable start and didn't run into any storms.

Running light helped. He'd be pushing things just to fly that high, but they'd serviced everything and he wasn't hauling a bomb load, so they should be able to fly through some of the passes without having to bounce over any mountains directly.

Zareen turned once and studied the situation and then nodded. She turned back to the truck driver and lit a small fire under his ass, from the way he bowed and spoke softly then immediately jumped into the truck. Gears got ground pretty hard and then he tore out like the Revenuers were on his tail and gaining.

"He'll contact one of the nicer hotels and have them send a car around for us," Zareen smiled. "As well as bring back supplies for the aircraft. I am looking forward to a shower and a hot meal, and then some sleep."

Finn nodded and went back to help Hans. They probably had an hour before the locals got organized and then he'd spent a quiet night in town as well.

CHAPTER TEN

Zareen found herself falling into a Scottish personality as they got to the hotel and got settled. Too much of Olivia MacQuaid coming to the fore, but that was a reaction to the locals more than anything. The Soviets were trying to turn them into a new thing call *Uzbek*, even though most of them saw themselves as Tajik.

Stalin drawing artificial lines on a map and enforcing them, like so many damned Europeans.

As a Persian, the locals looked at her askance, but they had been ruled by everyone at one point or another, including Mohammed's legions and Temüjin's. Today, it was Stalin's, but Persians were not necessarily welcomed.

But a rich Scottish noblewoman who spoke Tajik was a thing to be wondered at and feared just a little, so she used it, going so far as to let more of grandmother's brogue into her English, after all those lessons on elocution from father's tutors to make her sound London.

And it appeared to be working. They did not see her as Persian, but English. Scottish, but she wasn't about to try to explain the difference.

She preferred being fawned over, as opposed to resented.

They had settled at a hotel in town that specialized in Westerners. A few British functionaries and merchants. At least one Frenchman, from the words she had heard emerging from a salon as she walked past. Many Russians, but that was to be expected, as the Soviets sought to extend and strengthen their control over the region and its stubbornness.

They had gotten checked in, settled, and cleaned up when there was a knock at the door.

Zareen was settled on a settee with a glass of wine as Ghada answered it. They had been expecting Finn and Emad, not the group of men that suddenly burst into the room with guns.

"What is the meaning of this?" Zareen asked, still quietly at this point, although there were windows behind her open should she choose to scream. Asher would certainly hear it, even if nobody else did.

Seven men who looked like hirelings and thugs, carrying a mishmash of rifles and machine pistols. She wouldn't elevate them to the level of soldiers, although they seemed to be wearing similar enough outfits that one might squint and call it a uniform.

The eighth man seemed to be in charge. He wore a western style suit that might have been Soviet in nature, but Zareen supposed that it was an improvement over the European villain who wore a glossy, black leather trench coat to project his evil.

One of the goons closed the door. Two more gestured Ghada over next to Zareen on the couch, being fooled by her western-style jodhpurs and blouse. The two women ended up in the middle of the mess.

"I am Muhemmet Bughra," he introduced himself. "I wish to purchase your aircraft and crew."

Zareen studied the man. He gave the impression of being tall, but wasn't. Lean, perhaps. Black leather riding books to the knee, with a belted tunic jacket in tan. Soviet surplus, perhaps, but it was hard to tell.

Raw beard that made him look scruffy, but his black hair

was trimmed and under a Russian style budenovka cap with the ear pieces tacked up. She could even see where a red star patch had once been sewn on the front for at least long enough that the rest of the fabric around it had faded, leaving a darker patch in the center of his forehead.

The man spoke Tajik. Zareen answered in English with a hard edge of highland brogue to it, like she had summoned Grandma Olivia herself.

"What's the meaning of this, then?" she demanded.

"It is known that you speak Tajik, Lady Shirazi," he said carefully. "And your name is Persian, even if your passport is British," he replied without losing the smile from his face.

"The aircraft is not for sale." She shifted languages, aware that this man had done some level of spying to know those things in just the few hours they had been at the hotel.

"We could requisition it for the revolution then," he countered.

"Revolution?"

"We will drive Chiang Kai-shek out of China, mistress," Bughra said. "I am told that your plane is a German bomber."

So, a communist, then. Backed by the Soviets, most likely, against the Chinese Nationalists that held the coast.

"And what am I supposed to do to get home or to my destination if you steal my plane, Bughra?" Zareen asked in a sharp tone.

That seemed to wound him, so perhaps she was just dealing with a revolutionary and not a common brigand.

"Further, the aircraft was converted at the factory to a transport," Zareen continued. "The bomb bay was removed entirely and replaced with a smoking lounge for guests."

"I'm sure something can be managed," he sneered. "With your aircraft, we could entirely route the Chinese at Kashgar and drive them out of the basin entirely."

"Do I have a choice in the matter?" she asked now.

Ghada had remained calm, but the odds were too great,

even for her. Especially if the men were armed. Someone would get shot, and she'd prefer it was one of the men.

Well, actually all of them, but she'd start small.

"You do not," Bughra replied. "We started with you, so that your employees will behave when we go round them up. If your friend would care to join me, some of my men will watch you here while we get the others and explain things to them."

She nodded sourly. Not much she could do at the moment. Her Mauser might as well have been on the moon for all the good it would do her back in the bedroom in her luggage. Ghada had knives, but would not be able to get all of them quickly enough, even in a hallway.

Zareen would play this one carefully for now. Finn and Emad were both men capable of great violence when necessary, and Asher had apparently broken some of his programming as well in order to help her.

It would be messy, but she would find a way out of this.

And perhaps she needed to be more militant in her own life after this.

CHAPTER ELEVEN

Asher noted that the sound in the hallway was that of several men, but he didn't attribute malice until Emad opened the door and five men rushed into the room with firearms.

Ghada Attar was with them, thrust forward first into Emad's arms to throw both off balance, allowing the other men to point firearms at everyone.

Asher refrained from reacting, seated at a table off to one side. He doubted that the weapons these men were holding were capable of damaging his chassis, but now was not the time to find out.

The room was overfull. Finn had been seated across from Asher at the small dining table, but jumped up before freezing. Emad and Ghada moved to one side.

Five men, no, six men entered with weapons drawn.

Asher classified the group as brigands using the human scale, with a leader dressed slightly better and carrying a small pistol of Soviet manufacture instead of a larger weapon. Each of his friends in the room had at least one firearm pointed at them, including Asher.

"Which of you is the pilot?" the man in charge demanded in harshly accented English.

"That would be me," Finn spoke up. "What seems to be the problem?"

"All of you sit down," the man commanded. He gestured at Emad and Ghada. "You two on the couch. Pilot, return to your spot at the table."

The four sat. The six remained standing. Asher presumed that Zareen had already been captured prior to this, but he had registered no sounds out of the ordinary, so hopefully nothing bad had happened.

"Get the others and the woman," the commander ordered in Tajik.

One of the men immediately departed. Asher relaxed and began to study the humans around him for body language. They were in a political region known colloquially as Soviet Central Asia, with the region around Samarkand being reclassified as Uzbekistan more recently by the officials in Moscow, to separate them from nearby Tajikistan.

"You," the commander turned to Asher now. "Why do you wear a mask?"

"Oh, you don't want to see his face without it," Finn spoke up with a slow drawl. "Not much I can promise you in this world, but that's one everyone would be better off without."

"I was severely injured in a crash and subsequent fire during the Great War," Asher offered in Arabic, just to see who spoke the language this far northeast. At least the leader did from his nod.

And nothing Asher had said was a lie, even though this new Mark Eight form was capable of lying to humans outright, as well as injuring them in the pursuit of a greater cause that would aid all of humanity.

He wondered where brigands fell on that spectrum.

"Fine," the man said.

While he paused, two others shoved Zareen Shirazi into the room and closed the door.

Asher noted that the brigands had not taken the time to

disarm Finn or Emad, so he presumed Ghada was also armed. He could fight. Only Zareen might be without immediate weapons in a fracas.

"I wished to purchase your aircraft, in order to bomb Chinese forces in Kashgar," the man said. "She says that it is not for sale, so I will requisition it for now. Perhaps you will get it back later. Perhaps not."

Asher did not like the smile that came over the human's face. From his studies of the species, he rated the odds of the California Condor being returned to them at less than eight percent.

Presumably, then, violence at some level would be called for.

"I am Captain Muhemmet Bughra," the man introduced himself now. "Pilot, what is your name?"

"Finn Severijns. You do realize that it's been reconfigured, right? Got no bomb bay. And if you want to carry stuff on outside racks, you can't have much or the plane won't get over the mountains. I was already planning to fly low up the passes with this light of a load. Ceiling is only sixty-five hundred meters above sea level."

"We will find a way, American Severijns," Bughra replied. "And you will fly us there."

Asher noted the relaxed way that Finn shrugged.

"You wanna do that, you'll need to talk to Hans," Finn said. "He's the loadmaster. I just fly."

"Who is Hans?"

"Left him back guarding the plane," Finn said. "Don't sneak up on him or he might open fire and maybe fly away when he can't raise us on a radio. Man fought in the Great War and is a little twitchy at times."

Asher noted that Finn was spinning tall tales at this point, as Hans Fertig was anything but twitchy. Quite possibly dangerous, but that was a different matter. Hans would be outclassed by a group of brigands with surprise, Asher had no doubt.

"So you just intend to capture foreign tourists and hold them for how long?" Zareen spoke up now.

They had put her on the far end of the couch, beyond Ghada, which might keep her safest if things were required to become...ugly.

Who was this new entity, this Mark Eight that he had transformed himself into, that night in Cairo, that he might actually look forward to doing physical and emotional damage to random humans?

"A week, at most," Bughra replied, turning to her. "Enough time to bomb the Chinese army at Kashgar and return. After that, my forces will join with the Uighur Army and drive those bastards back to the coast once and for all."

Asher did not expect that the brigands would have been able to read the fine hints of body language that flowed between Zareen and Finn as they looked at each other. He could not have, but for twenty years spent studying such things to try to understand.

Somehow, each managed to reassure the other that they could get out of this situation safely if they waited until later, although Asher was not sure what gave each of them that confidence.

But at the same time, he had encountered few people in his time on this planet that had the makings of heroes. Or as great a hero. Both Emad and Ghada were exceptional people who might normally star in their own story, but for the light the other two cast.

But it warmed his electronic soul to witness such a thing.

Bughra turned back to Finn now.

"American, you will accompany me to the airstrip, where you will convince your friend to surrender peacefully, so that we can construct bomb racks for your plane," he announced. "None of you were planning to stay long, so we will simply make sure you are checked out of the hotel correctly and hold each group hostage against the other's behavior while we have you separated."

"And then?" she pressed blandly.

Bughra surprised Asher by bowing to the woman.

"After we have destroyed the Chinese, you will be free to continue on your journey, Lady Shirazi," he said.

"With or without my plane and crew?" she asked tartly.

"We will find a way to get you back to Persia, if necessary," he said, sounding a little less friendly now.

Zareen took her cue from that, so Asher sat and waited as well. Too much risk right now, and he did not really understand the movements that Ghada Attar studied and practiced on a daily basis well enough to emulate them. Perhaps that was an oversight he needed to rectify later, but they had more immediate problems.

"Now," Captain Bughra announced quietly. "You will all accompany me as we slip out the door and down the back stairs. If you behave, nobody has to get hurt, and hopefully you will all depart Samarkand peaceably in a week."

He gestured and the guards became more attentive. Asher rose smoothly and allowed himself to be led. His chassis would not be mistaken for human if someone were to grab an arm, so he needed to make sure that he did not provoke them at a time when the others might be at risk.

Plus, he wanted to know what plan Finn and Zareen had worked out in a single glance.

The wonders of humans never ceased to amaze him.

CHAPTER TWELVE

Finn kept his gripes to himself. He still wasn't sure how he was getting out of this one, but he'd have Hans to help soon. And a California Condor as an ally. Hell, if nothing else, he could roll the aircraft inverted just to pin somebody to the ceiling if they weren't prepared. Or bounce them off it with a snap dive.

Plus, every man this Bughra fellow had to carry along was that much less in bombs, so he'd probably think two of them would be sufficient.

They were in a canvas-covered truck now, driving away from the hotel. Zareen and Ghada had been politely loaded into the back of a car while the men and most of the goons were back here following.

Damn, but he felt like an amateur, falling for that trick. But at the same time, from the look in Emad's eyes, and especially Ghada's, the smartest thing he could do when all broke loose was to stay out of their way.

Besides, the idiots hadn't even thought to frisk him and Emad for guns. He was willing to bet that Ghada had a few muleskinners where she could get to them quickly, push come to shove. Might be one hell of a surprise party at some point, but not when the fools were all keyed up for violence.

Emad was stewing, so Finn tapped the man's foot with his own and nodded when Emad glanced up. Oh, yeah, he was pissed. But this wasn't the time nor the place.

Pretty quick, the truck took them to the strip, along with all their luggage and stuff. Too much noise for even the Kraut to sleep through, but Hans wouldn't automatically come up with a .303 ready to rain havoc on the locals, regardless of the bullshit Finn had been spinning earlier.

As they rolled to a stop, Finn looked at the leader fellow and got a nod, so he stood up and stuck his head out of the covered rear and hollered.

"Hans, it's Finn," he called. "Got some guests. Could you come out quiet for now?"

He tensed anyway, just in case Hans did go sideways anyway. He'd been in the war. He knew the scent of trouble on the air.

"Finn?" Hans yelled back. "Who are these people?"

"Comrades," Finn said loudly.

Technically it was even correct, since he figured they were Soviets. He wouldn't call them friends, even in jest. And a couple of them were getting their heads split open with rifle butts at some point, if it was up to him. Ghada might skin them alive first.

Finn could see as Hans opened the door and stood with one of the stolen British rifles just inside it. He stepped down to the packed sand and looked at the lights in his face.

Before Finn could warn him, punks poured out of the truck and charged, but Hans already had his hands up and waiting. Like Finn, he knew better than to try anything right now. Finn was surprised when someone closed up the plane and hustled the big Kraut into the back of the truck at gunpoint.

They were clear the hell out at the north end of things here, so it wasn't like there were any witnesses around, but the truck took off and drove.

Not far, but to a compound with a tall, adobe-looking wall

all the way around. Probably useful back in the days of arrows or black powder. Not worth a damn against anything big these days.

Everyone got exited and hustled into one of the several buildings inside. Sun wasn't coming up for a while, but Finn moved sure and calm for now. If nothing else, the Condor still had guns on all sides. If he was pissed enough, he could put the plane into a tight turn at low elevation and let Hans and Emad cut loose with those big MG-15s he'd inherited from the Germans along with the craft.

They'd probably run out of ammunition before they knocked the place down, but that wasn't the same as not trying.

Money. That was the impression Finn got as the group was all reassembled in what looked to be a salon of some sort. The place looked rough and humble outside, but that was a shell game, a three-card-monty someone was running, because there were fine chairs and furniture in here. Silk shades for the window. Fancy throw rugs he felt bad walking across, even without mud on his shoes.

Somebody said something and all of a sudden lots of guns were pointed at all the friendlies. And he counted maybe a dozen shooters.

"You are armed, American?" Captain Bughra asked, stepping close.

Someone must have noticed something.

"Am," Finn nodded. He pulled open his jacket and the man reached in delicately and pulled out the old Colt.

"Who else?" Bughra demanded.

Emad was smart and did the same, losing his Webley.

Finn amended that to *for now* as he watched. Hans opened his jacket and shook his head. Finn tensed as they turned to Asher. This was when it would get dangerous. He measured the distance to the back of Bughra's head and wondered if he could stop the man.

But Asher pulled open most of his robes, leaving only a linen shirt close to his skin. Steel. Whatever that part was.

He said something in Tajik, Finn was guessing, because the rest calmed down and ignored the women folk.

And all Ghada's knives.

"Now, then, we are in a quieter place, less likely to be interrupted," Bughra said.

He made a hand gesture and about half of the dozen goons left the room. Same guys as before were around, and just as heavily armed, but Bughra and his *guests* were all seated now. Finn wondered if he was leaving stains on the chair, but then he noticed that the place already looked at little torn up.

Had they requisitioned this place and didn't give a damn? Or chased off the previous owner and claim-jumped?

Food for thought.

Bughra addressed himself to Hans in English.

"Loadmaster, you have not heard the previous conversations," he said grandly, like he was on stage somewhere. "I wish to take your aircraft and bomb certain targets in Kashgar before returning here."

Nobody was expecting Hans to start laughing uproariously, least of all Finn.

Took the fellow a little time to get things comfortable again.

"From here?" Hans seemed to be holding in a fit of giggles. "Might as well drop paint on them."

"Why?" Bughra demanded, getting a little hot under the collar himself.

"At sea level on a perfect day," Hans said. "Perfect, mind you, we could carry three thousand six hundred kilograms of bombs and equipment externally. Using rockets to take off at that. You wish to fly over Erkeshtam Pass with bombs on rack?"

More giggles, but that was one of the reasons he put up with Hans's bad jokes and lousy cooking. Man could balance angels on the head of a pin to get takeoff weight distributed cleanly.

"This would be a problem?" Bughra asked.

Hans held up two fingers.

"The pass is above three thousand meters," Hans turned serious. "Ten thousand feet to the Americans and the British. The aircraft could maybe carry two two-hundred-kilogram bombs over that pass. Any more and you risk running into a wandering camel because you will be flying so low. On top of that, you would not be carrying any crew except Finn, me, and a bombardier, or you would have to reduce that to a pair of smaller bombs. What in *Gott's* name do you want to do that for?"

"The Chinese hold Kashgar," Captain Bughra said, also turning serious. "In 1933 and 1934, we tried to dislodge them with armies. I had several cousins killed in the fighting."

"We?" Asher spoke up now. "You are Uighur?"

The head snapped around and Bughra scowled. He muttered something under this breath, and then recoiled in surprise when Asher fired something back at him, apparently in the same tongue.

Finn kept his face serious, but nobody appreciated that the Durren had taught Asher just about every language spoken on Earth these days, along with hundreds of others long since gone, mostly so he could read ancient manuscripts as he came across then.

Seems like Uighur was one of those tongues. Useful, even if Asher could have kept that silent and followed conversations. Course, maybe they were speaking in Tajik, too. Wasn't like he could tell.

Then Hans got *mean*. Finn couldn't think of any other way to describe it than that.

"You, chief hoodlum," Hans said to the man in charge. Didn't quite snap fingers under the guy's nose, but felt close. "I like a challenge. You find me some bombs. Two hundred kilograms each. Maybe one hundred if you think you aren't man enough for the flight and have to bring all your gunmen with you. We will build racks for them, then go off and bomb people."

He paused just long enough that Finn knew what was coming. He smiled anyway when Hans dropped the line on Bughra.

"If you think you can manage something so simple, that is."

CHAPTER THIRTEEN

Didier was at least impressed with the transport. As near as he could tell, it was identical to the version that Shirazi had stolen, a Luftwaffe Heinkel H-111 of some sort, but this one had been modified somewhat as well. The wings were a different color, and he suspected that they were different from the original model. They felt longer, which would probably mean more volume for fuel. And better range.

The interior had been redone like a salon in back. He had studied the model when pursuing Shirazi, so he recognized where the bomb bay had been rebuilt for a pair of bench seats that were comfortable, with six chairs behind that and then space for cargo storage.

A useful, long-range aircraft like you might send diplomats around in. Or spies, considering his traveling companions. Bertrand was seated aft, taking advantage of his lesser social status to avoid sitting across from Konrad and Fraulein Reiher with her hungry smile, leaving Didier to face them alone, the bastard.

"Samarkand?" he repeated, just to make sure he had heard it right the first time.

"That is correct, Dr. Beauchêne," Konrad smiled. "Spotters

located the craft in Tehran and relayed it to us. They departed northeast so we were able to quickly alert others along the flight path."

"Why do you suppose she would go there, *Herr* Doctor?" Reiher asked.

"I presume your other spies were accurate when they said that she had found her prey, the Man With No Face, and that they have made common cause, Fraulein," Didier smiled back at her and wondered again what man would find such a masculine creature attractive. "He must have known something, or perhaps they captured him and forced him to divulge information. Do we know where they have gone from Samarkand yet?"

"We do not," Konrad said. "At present, we will land in Tehran in an hour and then spend the night rather than trying to make that flight in the darkness, when we do not trust that the natives or the Russians know how to handle an airport."

Didier shuddered at the prospect of staying in a strange hotel, where the woman might make demands. Why could she not turn her attentions to Bertrand or Konrad? Why did she have to smile at him like that?

"Are you prepared to pick up local forces in Central Asia?" Didier asked instead. "I cannot imagine the German government having that warm of relations with the Communists."

"There are various groups that have been inserted into the region *sub rosa*, Didier," Konrad nodded. "There is always a concern that the Communists in Moscow will attempt to invade China from the northwest, or to aid various groups already in place, so we must keep a sharp eye here."

Didier subsided. Too much unknown, and now he was haring off after that woman into the middle of Asia on the flimsiest of information. What could she have found?

Of course, last time it had been in Lisbon, when she suddenly found some clue that had sent her racing madly to Cairo, giving him the slip for weeks until he caught up with her, right before she went off into the desert after something. And now Central Asia?

What had the Man With No Face told her?

Idly, he wondered if there was perhaps some truth to the ancient fables of supermen living in the Himalayas, hiding in some impossible-to-reach valley and watching. If the Man With No Face was indeed such an alien, was he leading her to some base his people had hidden on this planet?

"What are you thinking, Doctor Beauchêne?" Reiher asked, her voice softening now to the point a man might mistake her for a woman in the dark.

"Is it a trap?" he asked, gesturing.

"A trap?" she responded, leaning forward and aiming her breasts at him like torpedoes.

"What did she learn from the man that immediately had them all flying tremendous distances, when rumors suggest that the man we have been after had been living in the slums of Cairo for twenty years?" Didier pondered. "And why Samarkand? It is almost a dead end, because I would expect you could have a safer flight to Peking via British India, rather than risking the northern route through the vast, empty wilderness of Mongolia and Siberia. What is there?"

"We shall find out," Konrad replied grimly. "They are ahead of us, but as you noted, there are fewer and fewer places they might go now, so we will catch them."

"And then?" Didier asked, just because nobody had spelled it out yet.

"We will find out what she knows," he said with a cruel smile. "And then probably kill her."

CHAPTER FOURTEEN

Finn studied the contraption. He had to give the local boys that much credit. They'd listened to what Hans had to say and built it almost exactly the way he specified. Finn just hadn't figured out if Hans wanted to dismantle and keep that frame for later, so he would have the ability to drop bombs on folks.

You never knew when Hans might get angry.

Sun was low in the southwest now. They'd been at it all day, cutting and filing and welding. Finn was standing off to one side with two taciturn guards standing well away from him with machine pistols handy. Captain Bughra was in the bombardier's seat aboard the plane with the windows open. Hans and a mechanic were under the left wing doing something.

"Release now," Hans yelled.

Finn watched.

"*Ja. Gut,*" Hans called before moving to the right wing. "And again. Yes. That will do."

Finn figured they had just managed to make it all work. Whatever the hell that meant. Maybe that they'd be strapping five-hundred-pound bombs on and taking off soon. Hard to tell.

Bughra emerged from the aircraft a moment later. He was a

little oily and a lot dirty from doing too much of the work himself today, while Finn mostly stood around and occasionally answered questions.

Weirdest kidnapping he'd ever been part of, that was for certain. No wealthy socialites on this one, either.

The local mechanic grunted something and went back to work on his frames. Hans and Bughra walked this way, forming a triangle with him. Hans was grinning.

Anybody who actually knew Hans Fertig would worry mightily about a grin like that on his face. But Finn didn't suppose anybody but him had that inside of a scoop.

"It will work," Hans announced like a proud papa. He turned to the Commie now and glowered.

"Where are my bombs?"

Bughra kinda flinched, as if he kept expecting to have to use a lash to keep Hans in motion, rather than a chain to keep him from dragging the bunch of them all over the damned place.

Finn didn't know what the ornery Kraut was up to, either, but knew the man well enough to play along when Hans got that wild hair.

"Coming," the man replied, somewhat taken aback by Hans. "They are being removed quietly from a local arsenal for delivery tonight."

"Excellent," Hans smiled. "We need dinner now and then they must refuel the aircraft and I will attach the bombs so I can calculate everything."

Bughra turned to Finn, maybe for help.

"He's the expert," Finn smiled. "I just fly. Studying the maps, Osh is about five hundred kilometers from here, then you turn south and follow the pass up, before turning left again. Maybe another five hundred kilometers from Osh to Kashgar as we have to fly it."

"But you have the range?" Bughra asked.

"It will be tight," Finn shrugged. "If we could land in Osh or Kokand I'd feel better, but we can do it if the winds are good.

Take us about three hours to get there. Maybe four. Same home. You planning to leave when? I'll need daylight from Osh to see what I'm doing. Especially in unfamiliar terrain."

"You are taking this well," Bughra said, maybe the slightest bit concerned finally.

"You've said you'll send us on our way after its done," Finn smiled at him. "The Kraut and I are just employees of the lady, so we don't care who we're flying for."

"Could you be hired away from her service?" the man asked.

Finn watched the man's hands. Those seemed to be where he gave himself away. Bughra was twitchy and nervous, but couldn't find the corners of the map to scan things. Finn figured that if he seemed too suddenly enthusiastic, the man might smell a trap.

"Doubt you could afford us," Finn shrugged. "Nobody shooting at us when we work for her. Doubt you could say the same thing, ya know? Do we even know what the Chinese army might have for anti-aircraft guns?"

"We do not," the man replied. "We were driven out in '34 and they have reinforced it some, but aircraft change everything."

"That they do," Finn agreed.

Personally, he thought the man was an idiot. Planes looked pretty and were expensive, but you still didn't own some piece of land until you could put a seventeen-year-old with a rifle on top of it. He'd learned that back when he was with the Expeditionary forces, before he got himself a better job.

Pretty show horses that never won any battles except public relations, but he wasn't about to tell this goober that. Man might realize he was buying a pig in a poke at that point, instead of getting his forces separated out where Emad and Ghada might cause trouble.

"The weather report is for clear skies tomorrow," Bughra said out of the blue. "That will help?"

"Cool would be nicer," Finn replied. "Makes the air heavier when we're trying to haul a load, but clear gets us there and back again."

"Then we will have dinner now," the Ruskie said with a smile. "And I will return with Fertig and we will have the aircraft ready for you to take off early tomorrow morning. If we cannot strike them at first light, then we need to hit mid-morning, when they will be relaxed."

"Can't promise you anything, Captain," Finn shrugged. "But we can get there and do this thing. Then we'll be on our way."

"Indeed, Severijns," he nodded. "We will handle matters then."

Finn didn't like the way the man smiled at that, but they had the guns right now.

That would change tomorrow, though.

CHAPTER FIFTEEN

Zareen had recovered from her rage at the situation. Ghada might die of old age still angry at this point, but such would make it all a learning experience, and that would help. Most likely, if they got out of this situation then Ghada would insist on Zareen adding several of the woman's cousins or nieces to form a more proper bodyguard detail, as some sort of strange troupe of ladies-in-waiting or something.

Finn's aircraft would determine how many women might accompany them, assuming it was not destroyed by the Chinese shortly. Or confiscated by the local Soviet.

The invaders had left them alone in one wing of the palace they had apparently captured when the local kulak had fled, upstairs where they could not slip easily out a window with guards patrolling inside and out. Zareen had called a brief meeting with the others in the suite the Captain had assigned her and Ghada, so the four of them sat around a table with tea. Three of them, at least, although Asher had a mug in front of him slowly cooling, just to look like he drank. It was only half full anyway.

"What can we deduce from their behavior?" she asked in a

voice that would not carry even so far as the door, let alone listeners.

"Tajik tribesmen," Asher said. "Lately converted to the Soviet cause, but for most of them it was a matter of following their tribal leader in the form of Muhemmet Bughra. If he were a fascist, they would be wearing swastikas instead."

"Not ideologically committed, except for him?" she asked to Asher's nod. "Useful to know. Ideologues are the most dangerous types of men, because then anything can become acceptable behavior."

"Will they send us on our way?" Emad asked, serious before breaking into a smile. "I appreciate that you have had some good experiences with guerrilla forces before now, but I cannot read these men."

Zareen shared his smile. Emad's troops had captured her and the others at Gabal El Uweinat when she first went seeking the origins of the Man With No Face, who turned out to be a scholar sitting across the table from her.

"It teeters, Emad," she replied. "As Asher said, the men are not committed to a cause, except for their captain, so if he decides that dropping bombs on the Chinese is good enough, then perhaps."

"That one seeks revenge," Asher said. "A comment to himself when he thought no others could hear suggested that he had cousins who were killed previously at Kashgar, presumably in some revolutionary uprising, but I am unfamiliar with the recent history of this part of the world."

Zareen nodded.

"We will hopefully have a chance to see Finn, if not Hans, before they depart," she said. "These tribesmen are not particularly sharp or military, so whichever group does not have to face off with the captain will have an advantage. I presume their leader will be required to fly with the Condor, so we need to prepare for our escape here. Each of you start counting faces and routines, so we can estimate our opponents. Asher, how fast can you actually run, if pressed?"

She liked the way he sat back suddenly and drew a breath. Without lungs or human nerves, all of those were behaviors programmed into the man by the Durren to make him look and act more human.

He leaned forward again a moment later, conspiratorially.

"At present, perhaps a sustained speed of over sixty kilometers per hour," he murmured. "Faster over short bursts on level terrain."

"So if you had an opening, you could quickly escape and return with a vehicle?" she asked.

"Would we not be better off with the authorities?" Asher countered.

"We cannot presume that they would see Bughra as a criminal," Zareen said. "In spite of the situation, they might be working with him, especially if the man is a communist revolutionary working against the Chinese Republic just over those mountains. No, we must assume that we are on our own for now and get out of Samarkand at least, if not all of Central Asia. From Kashgar, we could head east and south and eventually make our way to one of many British colonies somewhere where we could have greater confidence in the law. Alternatively, we could backtrack to Persia and call on assistance there. I made a mistake in not assuming that the locals might be a problem, but I have spent too much time in Europe and Egypt lately, and forgotten myself. That will not happen again."

Asher suddenly placed a hand flat in the center of the table.

"A car comes," he murmured. "I believe it is the same one that transported you and Captain Bughra earlier, so he may have just returned."

Zareen nodded, still a little in awe at what this robot explorer could do when he put his electronic mind to a task. It was a shame that they had only made him a social geographer. Had he been a technologist, Asher might have been able to produce the sorts of weapons necessary to stop the fascists in their tracks and perhaps even save the world from another conflagration.

Of course, humans were a troublesome species. Zareen supposed that the capitalists and communists would come to loggerheads quickly enough. Already they were close, with so many capitalists engaging in fascist politics over the last decade or so.

"We will remain here," she decided aloud. "Ghada, could you put more water on to boil, presuming that we will have guests shortly?"

Ghada rose in the perfect silence she attained when focused and went to work.

It was still odd seeing her dressed as a western lady, rather than her preferred attire, but that had meant the difference between them thinking her a companion and a servant.

They had not disarmed her, although Zareen had seen the woman take on two intended muggers in a dark alley and beat them both senseless herself.

Asher rose and moved to a nearby chair, playing the role of the outsider scholar she had hired, a desert monastic type not given to food or drink with the rest. It made a useful cover.

They waited, small talk having largely evaporated.

Captain Bughra knocked and entered with Finn and a few guards with them. Bughra smiled when he saw the entire group together.

"Good, we will dine shortly and drink a few toasts to the success of our mission tomorrow," Bughra announced, gesturing Finn to enter and then standing in the door. "I will send a man for you in a few minutes."

He closed the door and Finn let go a heavy, angry sigh as he moved to the empty seat and Ghada placed a fresh mug in front of him.

"Hans is nuts," Finn announced in a quiet voice. "He's got it all working and is all set to go bomb Kashgar tomorrow."

Zareen was somewhat taken aback.

"Is that wise?" she asked.

Finn shrugged and drank some tea.

"Load will be an issue, so I presume it might just be the two of us and the Captain," he replied. "Anything more than that and I'm not sure we can get over the mountains at all. Be a bit iffy as is."

"But you'll do it?" she pressed.

That was when the hard look came into his eyes. The one that promised the sorts of violence that he had offered to Didier Beauchêne, back in Cairo that one night when the Frenchman and his assassin had captured her and Ghada.

For a moment, Zareen wondered if she was maintaining too high a profile, as people kept wanting to capture her to know what she knew or find out where she was going. This might be why her parents still considered her too young for the lifestyle she had chosen.

Was it time to actually grow up?

Perish the thought.

"I thought so," Zareen said to Finn, in answer to his unspoken comment. "We will prepare things here for your return, then."

That got a smile from the man. An ugly, savage smile, but about what she was expecting. Finn and Hans had flown together for several years before she met the men, taking care of themselves along the way.

They would do the same now, and she would just assume success somehow and plan for how she would deal with the men left behind.

All of this was just a sideshow to the map Asher had showed her, after all.

The map that might change the future.

CHAPTER SIXTEEN

Hans stood and smiled as he surveyed his handiwork.

Rough. Crude, even, but he was not a man to resist when some *schweinhund* wanted to hand him a gun. Or bombs.

He had been in the Great War, luckily as a snot-nosed mechanic because he had helped repair tractors before he was drafted. He remembered the poverty of the ground corps, forever having to make it work with whatever parts you had or could steal from someplace.

Only the officers with *von* in their names had ever eaten well. Or flown in aircraft that weren't hung together with wire salvaged from an old battlefield.

Hans had sent too many children up to die in their first week, a result of men with more ambition than empathy. If this latest fool wore a red star occasionally, it did not change what he was.

Fascist, Communist, Ritter, or Cossack, they were all the same. Men who had dedicated their lives to the assumption that they were born better than everyone else.

Finn had none of that silliness about him. That was the reason their partnership had worked so well. Perhaps he needed to get serious about getting an American passport one of these days. They would take him in, a *hund* of no great birth, without any complaints. Or the Swiss, perhaps.

Ze California Condor was ready to soar, this time equipped with a pair of deadly eggs that would be an unwelcome surprise for someone. Hans wasn't sure who Finn or Zareen would need to use them on, but that was not his job. He got the plane flying. Kept it in the air, especially after old *Cerberus* that had been a pain in the ass. *Und* when the Condor was not enough, he would help them steal a new one.

Hans looked around the stretch of sand and rock, sorry for once that they did not have a hangar they could have done their work in. More places to hide things, but the idiot tribesmen had looked at his mighty bird almost as a goddess, so they had not explored things as well as they should have. Nor searched it.

It also helped that he didn't speak Tajik and they didn't know any German or English. The two fools understood violence, and that was acceptable. They were guarding him after the truck had brought his two eggs and Hans had supervised three other men attaching them.

Just for the hell of it, he decided to have an entire conversation with the closest one. Young kid, barely off the farm. Or whatever they did around here. He remembered flying over fields irrigated in the middle of the desert, which was stupid, but nobody asked him. Hitler was just as bad.

"Hey, kid," he turned to the closest one in German first with a warm grin a meter wide, just to check. "Any idea how much I would enjoy kicking you in the balls and then stomping on your face?"

Big smile, so the kid returned it, nodding politely.

"Or how much fun I'd have fucking your sister right here in front of you and making you watch?" he continued in English, still smiling.

Kid didn't speak anything but Tajik, so that was good. Otherwise, he wouldn't be smiling back.

Well, maybe he would.

Hans had no idea what the kid thought of his family. If it was anything like the Mendelsohn side of the family, he might agree. Uncle Fritzie was just worst of that lot. How Hans's mother had escaped them was probably an epic for the ages, except that she didn't like Fritzie, either, which was why she'd convinced Papa to move to Mannheim.

But, he could at least mutter to himself for now, certain that they weren't understanding anything.

So he walked to the steps up and gestured the kid to follow, pantomiming walking up into the aircraft and heading up to the cockpit. He needed to check a few things now, before he caught some sleep.

Finn would want a fast pre-flight in the morning, especially if he was intent on actually getting there and then coming back afterwards. With or without bombs still on the wings.

If there was a way to get Fraulein Shirazi and the others safely away, he'd enjoy bombing the palace where they were apparently being held right now. Maybe strafing it a few times at low altitude, just to let him vent his spleen at those Russian Cossacks a little.

Pee all over them.

Kid followed him up the stairs and forward, slipping between the bench where a bomb bay had lived. Hans stopped him at the hatch with a hand, indicating all the places around where the idiot might touch something and break it.

Hans wanted to have a surprise tomorrow. The cockpit on the 111 was weird. Instead of side-by-side seats, this had a pilot on the left, like an American car. The navigator/bombardier/nose gunner could sit a little forward of the pilot, but to actually drop bombs or use the forward guns, he had to unbuckle himself and lie down facing forward.

Presumably, Hans would be relegated to a seat aft, possibly where the dorsal gunner sat when he was operating the radio instead of the guns. Not an aircraft well-suited to civilian use.

Hans wondered if he would convince Finn to swap such a

visually notorious aircraft for one of the new Douglas DC-3s he'd heard about. Slower than the Condor, and unarmed, but with the ability to carry a stunning amount of cargo in utter luxury, compared to *Cerberus* or this bomber.

Hans kept up a running commentary for the kid as he touched every gauge, every knob, and every control. Mostly just to put him to sleep, but partly to keep up a friendly patter. It all looked good at this point, and someone had even found him a weather report showing that things would be almost perfect.

Of course, it was summer. Hans could only imagine trying something this stupid in the dead of winter, when you might have to drive over the pass because the air wasn't giving you enough lift.

"*Sehr gut,*" he said as he rose, walking back towards the kid and gesturing for him to exit.

Fool did, too. No reason not to.

Hans took just long enough to confirm that his old Beretta M1934 was still tucked in where he had hidden it when they first bought the plane. He'd gotten it from a drunk Italian officer in trade for some "authentic Somali whiskey" he'd gotten from a Scotsman for a...What the hell had he gotten for the man?

Hans couldn't remember. Wasn't that important, except that it had gotten him the pistol, tucked safely away.

Hans followed the kid down the steps before the boy realized that Hans wasn't right behind him.

Nice kid.

Hans would be happy if the punk got left behind tomorrow.

The Russian he'd shoot without any qualms.

CHAPTER SEVENTEEN

Asher listened as the others went to sleep, each having locked their doors, as much good as it might do when Uighur Captain Muhemmet Bughra probably had the key. But the man had posted guards at the end of the hallway, at the top of the stairs, quietly instructing them not to bother anyone and to just keep watch.

Asher presumed that the man was unaware that he had a spy in the building. One who could actually turn up the gain on his external microphones sufficiently and filter the rest of the noise out to hear what the man said. Little of it had been of any great value, but Asher was used to recording a dozen separate conversations around him at once in a coffee shop or tea house, isolating each for informational value that he could trade with other merchants in Cairo.

Bughra did not seem to be a man with ultimate betrayal in mind. That did not mean bad things might not happen tomorrow, but Asher was preparing for the possibility of repeating his outrageous activities stopping a mugger, in which he had actually done physical damage to a human, in the course of protecting an older human male in the process of being beaten.

He just had to look at humanity as a separate object from

humans. If he did that, he could see them as a thing to be protected, judging certain humans less important than others because of their activities.

Already, his ethical programs complained loudly but harmlessly, noting that the road to hell was paved with good intentions, such as the humans might classify it. Planning to do harm was an evil the Durren scientists who built him thought they had prevented. But weren't they criminals, for illegally deploying an A.S.H.E.R. unit on this planet in the first place?

His circuits would not allow him to indulge in the mysticism of angry gods striking them down in retribution, but the chances of his ship having been destroyed in such a manner that Asher alone survived was already so far down the path of standard deviations that it was hardly worth considering. Maybe someone really had angered some human gods.

So he listened to the guards. They were rotated out roughly every ninety minutes and replaced with others. If the pattern held, they would do the same tomorrow.

At some point, men would be sent to retrieve the party for breakfast. Asher would claim a few rolls and conceal them about his robes for the others, still maintaining the illusion that humans would be disgusted by his scar-burned face. It had worked, and the Tajik tribesmen loyal to Muhemmet Bughra would have no reason to doubt it.

Outside, other guards maintained a casual but ongoing patrol around the inside of the compound, with a few electric lights illuminating the courtyard and walls. Asher had read many human treatises on military strategy and tactics. Few, however, gave him the necessary tools to estimate the best way forward, but he had several friends with greater expertise on the topic, so he would rely on them.

Him, the sociologist who might turn into the warrior, because he could not be easily harmed by the weapons at hand, and could thus protect the others, from even the tribesmen, as he could strike them in such a way as to render them unconscious without much risk of accidentally killing anyone.

Ghada would not be so restrained. Nor would Emad.

He would lead. He would protect them.

He would even guide Zareen Vüsala Shirazi to what the maps indicated was a hidden and supposedly abandoned Durren base. Perhaps a forward staging observatory for scholars studying the ancient cultures of south and east Asia, in an earlier millennia.

How else was he going to save the world?

CHAPTER EIGHTEEN

Finn heard the key hit the lock and sat stone cold sober upright before the door finished opening. And he hadn't even had anything to drink.

Too much time spent in cheap hotel rooms where thieves might break in and need to be punched before they made off with all your stuff.

"Ah," Bughra said. "You are awake. Are you ready?"

Finn shrugged and slipped his feet into his boots, lacing them rather than give the guy the ragged edge of his tongue. He stood and studied the Captain.

Shorter, but he gave the appearance of being bigger. Personality, mostly. Intellect. Plus he'd been pretty well fed as a kid, compared to the scrawny boys with rifles guarding the place, so he had an extra two inches on them. None of them likely fought in the Great War, or even against the Whites later.

Finn had managed to get himself demobilized before he got sent on to Russia, but he'd heard stories about what that one had been like.

It was just another war for one's homeland. He could give them that. Bughra hadn't even been much of an asshole, beyond the initial jump. That Frog in Cairo had been worse.

Thank God he'd finally managed to get himself lost and would not be bothering them anymore.

Finn's jacket hung on a chair. He grabbed it and slipped it on for now, but he'd need to change into something heavier when they got to the plane. Bughra was already dressed pretty warm, so he knew what would be coming.

"Let's do this," Finn nodded.

Bughra had two goons, but no pistol in his hand, so they were all going to play this like a simple hand-off. Finn had been around a few of those, but only participated once. That one time outside Muskegon.

One gang had captured a couple of lugs running moonshine through someone else's territory. To get even, the other gang kidnapped someone's teenage kid. Before things had gotten out of hand, a trade was set up, everyone looking tough and ornery, but behaving.

There were rules. Laws were something else, but most of the underworld followed a set of codes that were almost as predictable and good enough that civilians didn't get hurt in the crossfire.

So he was a prisoner. Hopefully the trade value was in him bombing a bunch of Chinese strangers for no other reason than the gun to his head.

Finn figured he'd have to sell this plane after that and find something else to fly. It was already a little notorious around Egypt and the eastern Med. This would make it a worldwide pariah.

He fell into step with the guy. Down the hallway and past the guards, walking quietly enough that nobody but Asher probably heard. Maybe all of them if they were awake, but they were locked in for now and Bughra didn't look like the type for weepy, emotional send-offs, even if there was anybody in the group that would go down that path.

Down to the ground floor and out the big double doors onto the covered porch. The car was waiting. Four of them got in and the driver at least managed to not grind the gears that badly getting them in motion.

"You are taking this well," Bughra said over the noise of the engine and road.

Finn shrugged.

"Not a lot of choice in the matter, is there?" he asked, turning to look at the man.

"Not really." Bughra gave him a sad smile. "But it will be over and done soon and we will go our separate ways."

Finn studied the man, but didn't smell a trap or a double-cross coming. And he didn't have much to say, so they fell into a surly kind of silence for the rest of the ride. Neither of the gunmen in here were dressed for high altitude in a tin can, so he might be turning the tables on Captain Bughra soon.

He could wait.

Fast enough, they pulled up to the Condor, lit already by a couple of cars parked facing forward. Hans was up and dressed, waiting patiently.

Bughra and his gunmen got out first. Finn followed.

"Gear is aboard for you," Hans said as they walked close. Man ignored Bughra entirely when he said it, too.

Wasn't much. A boilersuit that he'd picked up like the one Hans was wearing right now. More surplus that had fallen off the back of a Royal Air Force truck somewhere, but Hans handled that stuff and Finn had learned a long time ago not to ask.

And if Bughra wanted to freeze his ass off, that was his choice. The alternative was sitting aft in the passenger compartment where there were heaters drawing air off the engines. It could be pleasant back there, but the nose had occasionally been chilly even in Egypt. Heading into the mountains of Central Asia, it had gotten downright cold up there a few times.

"How's the load?" Finn asked, studying today's cargo.

He'd never actually dropped bombs on people. Empty beer bottles didn't count, technically. Full ones might have.

"You will fly forward and nose heavy," Hans announced with great surety. "The autopilot will drift because I did not take the time to adjust it backwards, so do not rely on it for vertical. It will still hold the lateral just fine."

Finn nodded.

Always sounded like a different man speaking when he did that, but Hans was the best at that sort of thing. Give him a jigsaw puzzle cut into a thousand pieces and he'd have it done in an hour or two at the most. Challenge him to pack too much stuff into too small a space and then get the hell out of his way when he went and did it.

Finn turned to Bughra now and studied the man.

"Is this really necessary?" he asked, grim but willing to go through with it.

"It is."

'Bout what he figured.

Zareen would either have to skip Kashgar after this, or find a new airplane that the Chinese Army wasn't going to shoot on sight.

He'd deal with that tomorrow. Right now, he studied the stars in the chilly night sky and did the math. Preflight and such, and he'd just about be ready to roll up the runway as the morning was lit enough to actually see what he was doing.

Hell of a way to start a morning.

CHAPTER NINETEEN

Didier was dressed up a step today, in the finer brown suit he had brought with him when he left most of his wardrobe and such in storage at the German embassy in Cairo. At least no one would steal it, but he would be required to ask the Germans to get it all back. Probably that would require Schwarzenberg and Reiher be alive accompanying him.

Or a really good story about their demise and how he had barely managed to escape with his life.

He looked across the space to where that damnable Fraulein sat and smirked at him. The engines were running hard and loud, making conversation somewhat difficult, which was a relief.

She had dressed for the chase as well today, if you wanted to call it that.

Gray riding jodhpurs that seemed too small, such that they were almost skin tight and tucked into black leather riding boots. She had a double-breasted coat that matched, but had left it folded over a chair in back, so she could show off a white shirt that should normally be buttoned up higher than the button on a line with her nipples.

Reiher's cleavage seemed to be aimed at him like a trap this morning. Didier knew that Bertrand liked Rubenesque women, but he could not bring himself to find her attractive. Certainly the face was beautiful enough, and the wavy blond hair did not distract all that much.

Didier simply preferred the whippet to the rottweiler.

Schwarzenberg was in a uniform that looked like German Luftwaffe with all the badges removed. Or never sewed on. Gray jodhpurs but baggier. Gray tunic jacket with a shiny leather belt. He even had a saucer hat inverted on the bench next to him as he sat and quietly read a book that Didier hadn't noted the title of before now.

"What would you have done, had you been successful before now, Doctor Beauchêne?" Reiher asked, uncrossing her legs to lean forward in such a way that for a moment he was certain he could see her navel.

Didier focused on her eyes and kept himself from grumbling at the woman. Or from matching her forward stance. That would put their faces perhaps thirty centimeters apart. Useful for conversation in the noise of the aircraft, but he could already smell her perfume from here.

He composed a thought and studied her.

"Overthrown the Third Republic and instituted a fascist one to replace it, in much the same manner as Mussolini or Hitler," Didier replied. "A Third French Empire, as it were, perhaps like the first Bonaparte, but more likely a Fourth Republic of some sort, since we would need leaders to guide the fools into a more modern understanding of their place."

"And the Man With No Face?" she asked, still focusing her charisma and physical assets on him in a manner that made Didier concerned that she was about to climb into his lap. Or pull him into hers.

"Both Shirazi and I are convinced that he is an alien," Didier said. "That the event in 1916 was an accident of some sort that left him stranded on Earth, unable to contact his fellows. He wears a mask so no one has seen his flesh. He is known to sit in a cafe for hours without consuming any coffee or tea, when the average human is constantly sweating and needing to replenish fluids. No one has ever seen him eat."

"And had you captured him, such as Shirazi seems to have done?" she pressed, pupils dilating with some unspoken excitement.

"If I am right, then he has come here from another planet," Didier told her. "Mars. Venus. Perhaps another solar system entirely, although Einstein's equations might prove that impossible. But a technology far in advance of ours. Imagine unstoppable armies sporting super weapons."

"And what would you do with such armies?" She cocked her head now.

Konrad glanced up as well.

"Destroy the British," Didier sneered. "Perhaps take their Empire away from them. Then the Russians and their stupid experiment in Marxism."

"And Germany?"

"France has its colonies," Didier said. "Germany should have some as well. Perhaps space carved out of Russia on that flank, since they are hardly using any of it now. Reclaim Danzig and East Prussia. Who knows? The key is that fascism is the future of humanity, so Germany, Italy, and a reborn France need to lead the way."

He was not so stupid that he missed the glance that passed between those two as she finally sat back on her bench and crossed her legs again. The Germans were assisting because they needed him to sniff out the alien, but Didier expected them to try to cut him out of the deal when they got there.

Germany needed an Empire, certainly, but they could rip it out of their eastern frontier like wolves, rather than the west. The Rhine made an acceptable natural frontier between the cultures. Let the Slavs suffer under Nazi rule while his Fourth Republic took all of Africa. It was larger and had more resources to exploit, anyway.

"How soon until we arrive in Samarkand?" he asked, glancing back and forth at the two.

Reiher turned to Konrad to speak, so the man closed his book with a finger to mark a page.

"The direct distance is about twelve hundred kilometers," Konrad said. "As we are not pushing the aircraft hard, I am informed by the pilot that we should arrive in the early afternoon, perhaps just after lunch. I have wired ahead and we will be contacted by a local agent when we get to our hotel. From there, we will determine where they have gone next, but I expect they only have a day's head start on us now, so they will be run to ground soon enough."

"So they will be gone?" Didier felt deflated, but he had been dueling with Shirazi for more than three years at this point, neither able to gain much of an advantage on the other.

"They did not spend long in Acre, nor Tehran," Konrad smiled grimly. "I do not expect them to remain in Samarkand. And they are heading northeast, because if they were headed into the Soviet Union, they would have probably gone to Istanbul from Acre, or either Rostov or Volgograd from Tehran. Either they are headed to northern China, or the Man With No Face is taking them into Siberia, possibly via Novosibirsk or Irkutsk."

Didier nodded. He had come to the same conclusion, but he also knew that both of those Siberian towns would be stepping stones if one were headed to Tunguska, site of an event on 30 June 1908 that nobody had adequately explained to date.

Another crashed and exploded spaceship? The Libyan desert seemed to be a place where the Man With No Face had originated.

Was there a war being fought between two sides in outer space? One group that wanted to invade and exploit a colony on Earth, in much the same manner as the French government ruled Algeria, possibly with a second group preventing them?

Was there a war being fought in deep space for control of Earth itself?

All the more reason to gain access to such alien technology, in order to protect his planet.

But he did not mention that to his *associates*. If he could call them that. Schwarzenberg and Reiher had their secrets from him, so he would keep things from them, at least for now.

After all, not many people even knew about the Tunguska Event, outside of a small circle of scholars and astronomers, neither of which described the two across from him.

But if they were headed deep into the East Siberian taiga, they would need to tread carefully. Perhaps even recruit a full expedition, because the boreal forests would be full wilderness, with no bases and few people. And they would require coordinates, if they were going to locate a runway where they could set down this aircraft.

What are you up to, Shirazi? How much do I tell my new friends, and how much do I leave as a surprise for them?

Didier wondered if he might even end up using the British princess to kill the Germans for him. The world did not need Hitler's Reich. In fact, a new French social and political revolution might be the thing to shatter Germany back down into the mess it had been before Bismark had assembled the modern state a lifetime ago.

Perhaps he really needed to become a new Bonaparte after all, expanding a French Empire to the borders of the Soviet Union.

And beyond.

CHAPTER TWENTY

Zareen had stood at the door and listened, but not made any noise. She'd hardly slept, but that was normal. Finn and Hans were in trouble because of her, and she needed to find a way to rescue them. They wouldn't be here except for her unquenchable desire to know the truth about Asher's people.

Ghada shared a small suite with her, two bedrooms off of a sitting room, presumably for important guests. Her door was open, and Zareen knew the woman was probably sitting on her bed in a lotus, meditating, but prepared for violence at the first need. Thus had she always been.

Breakfast would be forever in getting here, but it was only a few hours past midnight right now and she needed to plan.

Footsteps went past and away. Finn or the Tajik hetman murmuring quietly, guards answering just as low as she listened at the door.

Asher and Emad were across the hall and down some. Finn had been on the same side.

Zareen knew that there were guards on her left if she were to stick her head out of the doorway. They had a clear view of this wing and there would be no sneaking past them. Similarly, by putting the prisoners on both sides of the hallway, they could not all escape without some coordination that would be heard.

She would strike mid-morning. Most of the guards would be awake, save for the crew that had been up all night, but there was no other way to do this. If she waited too long, Finn might complete his mission and return. Or he might have disarmed or disabled Captain Bughra and be ready to assault the compound directly.

Or drop bombs on it. Better if she and the others were elsewhere, to give him that option. Plus, he might be able to do something as soon as they got in the air and out of immediate sight, so she needed to move.

And it would be time to return to Persia soon. Bring Ghada's sister and cousins. A whole cast of ladies-in-waiting, as it were. That would limit her flexibility, having more people to account for, but it would allow her to have people who had no other job but to keep watch. Ghada did more, and Zareen demanded things that had gotten her captured a second time.

She was in no mood to try for a third.

Zareen turned to Ghada's open door and stood there.

An eye opened, but Ghada gave no other indication that she even breathed at this point, such was her mastery of the esoteric fighting arts she had learned from her kin in the western mountains.

Zareen moved to the foot of the bed and sat carefully, so as not to cause the springs to squeak and ruin the perfect silence.

Ghada opened her eyes now and studied her.

"After breakfast, I will cause a distraction," Zareen informed her. "Here, in the room, just as they are preparing to lock us in again. You will disable the guards that come to see. Asher will go after the reinforcements. You and he will then begin disabling the men, preferably without killing any more than are necessary for us to escape."

Silence.

"Some, then," Ghada finally replied.

"Presumably," Zareen agreed. "We cannot assume that they are so foolish as to come at you one at a time where you might chop them, but I would like to leave Samarkand with as little blood feud as possible."

Ghada smiled. The men had seen her practice. Seen her dance those slow movements that did not look deadly until you sped them up and they turned into punches, kicks, blocks, and death-dealing.

Asher was still faster, but he would use simple fists, steel clubs covered by leather gloves.

They would take everyone down, and then escape.

It would be that simple. Hopefully the tribesmen wouldn't expect it today, since they had promised to release everyone in a few days.

And if you'll believe that, my friend, I have a bridge in New York City to sell you, as well.

CHAPTER TWENTY-ONE

Finn brought the power up smoothly. The Condor was playing nice today, like she knew what was coming and had decided to go along with it. Not like some horses, where you had to get out the bucket of oats and maybe a carrot or two to get them to stop bouncing around.

He was mid-left, in the pilot's seat. Hans was in the navigator/bombardier seat, forward right, where he normally sat when he wasn't flying. There was a seat more or less behind Finn, flipped down so a third person could be up on the flight deck.

Like now.

That one had a pistol, but Finn wasn't all that offended. Bughra hadn't been a prick about it. Almost apologetic, as a matter of fact.

But he was still holding them hostage to a mission Finn wouldn't have taken otherwise. Muskegon, all over again.

But that was okay. Bughra had taken Finn and Hans at their words that a fourth crew member would be too much, with the drag and weight of those two bombs down below. If the weather behaved, he'd be able to get over the pass easy enough.

Finn knew, however, that there was going to be someone at Erkeshtam Pass likely to see a Heinkel H-111 with bombs on external racks and draw the obvious conclusion. They'd call the closest base on the radio and Finn would be flying into a sea of machine gun fire by the time he got over whatever base the Chinese Army had close by Kashgar.

He sure as hell wasn't about to bomb a city, thank you very much.

So he needed altitude. Lots of it.

Although, come to think of it, what would it be like if they kept those racks and added external fuel tanks of some sort instead of bombs? Probably increase the range pretty far, even after costing them for fuel economy. Was that why that damned Kraut had agreed so readily?

Finn wouldn't put it past him. Not Hans.

Finn finished touching everything with fingertips and mind. Condor was ready.

He turned and looked at Bughra.

"Permission to launch?" he asked in a sardonic voice.

After all, he'd be a serious war criminal in some circles if he did this, various treaties be damned. He wanted to be able to say that a man had been holding a gun on him the entire time and threatening to shoot him otherwise.

Might not save his ass, but maybe it would look good when the judge was deciding a sentence.

St. Peter was likely to be a little pissed, but all things considered, Finn wasn't even sure something like this would make the top ten list when he was standing before the man. Hopefully, he'd have a lot of chances to make up for it between now and then, because he sure hadn't been shriven in a while.

Bughra nodded and even smiled wanly, like he was reading Finn's mind. Hopefully not, so that they could lull the bastard to sleep at some point and flip the script on its head. Preferably without everyone getting killed in the process.

Finn brought the throttles up and listened to the power course through the whole frame. Smooth. Condor knew it was race day and had calmed right down.

Sun was thinking about coming up soon. Maybe another fifteen or twenty minutes. At least he was headed a little north of east this morning, so he wouldn't be staring directly at it as it rose. Condor was still all glass nose, with no easy way to avoid the sun.

Best he could do right now would be to get to altitude and set the autopilot, but watch it like a mother hen until he understood what it was going to do with the different center of gravity.

Finn checked all directions, and the ground crew had backed way off, so he had lots of space to work. Nobody coming in, either, which was good. All his running lights were on, but Finn knew better than the trust that the other guy was going to do a proper approach with a downwind before landing. Stupid git just might land direct if he was coming from the north, all lined up with the runway.

Finn opened the engines and let the beast howl. Tail came up pretty quick, but it always did. Finn let her run a little extra today before pulling back on the stick and leaping into the fading night sky.

He was used to busier airstrips, where there might be planes coming in, having flown all night and needing either the lights turned on or someone to drive some trucks out to show the strip. Zareen was taking him farther and farther from that, so he was going to have to get used to working with less and less support where he landed. External fuel tanks and maybe it was time to steal or buy some better tools and equipment. Maybe stock spares of things against replacement time, too.

World was getting weird when he was going to have to place orders with the Luftwaffe third-hand through a broker. Or fence.

The Condor rose smoothly. Hans watched. Finn flew. He didn't bother to glance back, but he presumed that Captain Bughra and his pistol were back there watching everything.

Nothing was going to get stupid right now. That was later. If he was lucky.

"Zero-Seven-Five," Hans announced, just to repeat himself, in case Finn hadn't been listening an hour ago, or had forgotten.

But the big Kraut had his own nervous habits when flying, so Finn wasn't insulted.

"Zero-Seven-Five," he replied, matching the nose to the compass.

There was a road to Jizzakh, but it didn't take him where he wanted to go. This route would cross him south of Khujand and then Kokand, on the way to Osh, where they would turn south and cross technically over into China.

And where Finn and the California Condor would go to war.

CHAPTER TWENTY-TWO

Zareen had watched carefully, but she had not been surprised. With Captain Bughra gone, the men were more relaxed. Less disciplined. If the man was going to be gone for longer than a day, she might have concerns for herself and Ghada, but the leash would not slip immediately.

They were at breakfast. The tribesmen had obviously eaten, at least the half of them currently watching from around the room. Zareen sat with Ghada, Emad, and Asher at a table that could feed twenty in a pinch, in a formal dining room done in dark woods and white stucco. It shouldn't work, but someone had balanced the dark floor and ceiling beams with two walls paneled and two painted white. There were double doors that opened onto a rear courtyard, with two men inside guarding it and two more outside.

"How did everyone sleep?" she turned to Emad and smiled.

"As normal for the desert, when there is a strange aircraft involved," he replied in a low voice, holding a coffee mug in such a way that nobody could read his lips.

Zareen nodded. Like the time Emad and his band had snuck up on her and Finn then captured them all. They had missed his base when flying in, but he had heard *Cerberus* overhead.

It had turned out much better than she imagined possible.

So he had not slept much, or perhaps had then roused early to prepare mentally.

"Asher?" she turned to her other "male" companion.

"I meditated and listened to the universe speak to me," he said lightly.

Zareen understood those implications as well. And he had apparently not heard anything bad enough to warrant taking action on his own. Good to know.

"Personally, I have not been feeling all that well," she said louder than necessary for the small table, just in case anyone here spoke English. "After breakfast, I plan to take a nap and see if that improves anything."

Emad had a look of sudden concern that melted her, but then his eyes turned shrewd and he nodded ever so slightly.

She glanced at Asher. It took him a moment longer before he also nodded, but he lacked the human chemistry to understand her kind, and had to make do with what he had learned. Granted, the man had lived in Cairo as an information broker for decades, but that did not necessarily prepare him for a life of adventure.

Breakfast was dull. Rolls and a porridge, but that was fine today. Asher had claimed several rolls for himself, *to eat later*, and those would be snacks for the others when they succeeded in freeing themselves, if they found it necessary to run.

Zareen still had hopes that she might be able to capture the dozen or so men remaining in the compound, after a small group had gone to wait at the airstrip.

Time would tell, so she drank a heavy, dark coffee and felt it energize her for what she had to face.

The others were all older than her. Ghada by six years. Emad by more than a decade. Finn and Hans by nearly two decades. And yet they deferred to her. Expected her to solve the situation and lead them to victory.

So she would.

The others had finished eating as well, so she sat and enjoyed the last of the coffee before nodding to Ghada and rising. Immediately, the two guards on the inner door perked up, prepared to escort them all back to their rooms and watch them there, as they had done yesterday.

Zareen stumbled a little and put her hand to her forehead. Ghada caught her and slipped a hand around her waist to told her up.

Zareen went ahead and slumped more of her weight on the solid woman, playing the tired, perhaps ill noblewoman.

"What is wrong with her?" the closer guard asked in Tajik.

"She is not feeling well," Ghada replied sternly. "Do you have a doctor? Can you get one out here?"

Zareen looked up and kept her face neutral and maybe a little pained. The young man with the machine pistol paled. He didn't look like a sergeant. Captain Bughra didn't have any older men that might provide training cadre for a small military unit.

The tribesmen looked like people Muhemmet Bughra had grown up with, back in his tribal homeland, and then recruited to join him when he became a Soviet. It made him an officer, but didn't provide his men the tools they needed to think without him.

"No," the tribesman stuttered.

Zareen guessed him to be perhaps twenty-four, and the sort where Samarkand was the big city that still made him nervous.

"Get one, then," Ghada ordered the boy. "I will take her to her room to lie down."

Ghada turned to the other one now and actually snapped her fingers at him to get his attention.

"You," she called. "Lead us while this one gets help."

They reacted to authority. Lacking Bughra, Ghada filled the

role a sergeant would have, telling them what to do. The first one turned and trotted out of the room, presumably to call someone or drive into town. The second swallowed, nodded, and immediately led them back to the staircase and up. Asher and Emad trailed quietly. The other two guards stomped more noisily.

Zareen moved slowly, leaned on Ghada such that she could whisper in the woman's ear.

"In the room, where you can trap them in place," she said quietly.

Ghada nodded, still holding enough of her weight to make the scene believable.

The stairs were a slow haul, just because Zareen wanted to give that first boy time to get out of earshot. Hopefully, out the front door and racing madly into town to fetch a doctor, if she could be so lucky.

The other boy led and two more trailed.

They reached her door and the boy entered after opening the door. Zareen let Ghada haul her into the sitting room and then to her bedroom. Asher and Emad entered as well, so the other two did.

"You, help me get her onto the bed," Ghada ordered, still in fluent Tajik.

The young man slung his machine pistol across his back and stepped right up to do whatever the older woman in charge ordered him to do.

"Can you stand up?" Ghada asked in a simple voice, pushing Zareen to her feet.

Zareen came upright and pulled her hands in against her body, standing perfectly still so as not to intrude.

Ghada turned with a smile and punched the young man in the belly so hard he folded in half around her fist and collapsed.

CHAPTER TWENTY-THREE

Ghada felt the grains of sand slow as she moved. It was always like this when she became focused on combat.

The arts had originated in ancient China, and then been carried by merchants and scholars over the passes and deserts of the ancient Silk Road to Persia. Most travelers had not given such things much thought, because they were intended for a culture where weapons were not generally allowed to the peasantry, carried to lands where the ranks of the nobles wore heavy armor and carried swords.

Those days had passed, and now most people wore no armor at all, relying on firearms instead.

Her first target collapsed. Possibly unconscious, but more likely winded for a time. Long enough for the mistress to disarm him.

Asher had lashed out with a metal fist, clubbing one man awkwardly, but with enough strength to knock him down. Again, possibly out. At least concussed.

Emad had foolishly grabbed the other and was wrestling with him. Ghada flowed close and hammered the boy in the kidneys twice with fists. He wasn't much taller than her, so she grabbed a handful of hair when he started to pitch over backwards, driving a fist carefully into the spot just behind and below the ear where all the nerves cluster nicely.

This one was unconscious, and would remain so for a while.

She wanted to check the other one—Asher's foe—but time was critical. They had surprise right now, and would until someone cried loud enough or began firing shots.

Ghada smiled as she considered her options. She had been approaching this like a military campaign, but Musashi had also been brought to Persia in his writings.

The mistress and Emad were disarming foes. But weapons would just lead to a firefight.

Instead, Ghada had an idea so utterly goofy that nobody would expect it. Or be able to properly counter it.

She unbuckled the silly Western-style belt, then pulled her dress over her head, tossing the slip and chemise with it. Shoes off. Brassiere and panties went onto the pile, along with three knives. Emad stared at her stunned. Possibly Asher as well.

"I assume you have a plan," the Mistress observed, holding a machine pistol as Asher began ripping a blanket to make bindings and gags.

Emad al-Sadri might hurt himself, the way his jaw had fallen completely open.

"Asher, I will need your speed," Ghada said quietly. "Emad, you will capture prisoners as I disable them. Mistress, you will remain here as a command post."

Zareen nodded, but Ghada had been with her for over a decade. Asher tore the rest of the blanket, enough for eight men, and then stepped up. al-Sadri eventually managed to close his mouth, even if his eyes were too big.

She smiled. Exactly the response she was needing from these foolish Tajik bumpkins.

"I will lead," she said quietly. "Asher, you will remain close. Emad, you will watch our flanks and rear back behind a gap. Questions?"

None.

Ghada nodded and walked right out into the hallway as though she owned the building and everyone in it.

Nudity was not a taboo to her people, but these were back-country boys come to the big city. It would confuse them to no end. Distract them. Tantalize them.

Who would imagine a woman like her, completely nude, might be dangerous, after all? Bughra wasn't here to see through it.

She glanced back and nodded as the two men emerged.

Down the stairs and into the main hallway. Ghada figured she would take the ones that had been cooking and would be cleaning right now. They had access to knives and could warn the others. Best to eliminate them immediately.

She reached the door to the dining area and found it empty. Nobody stood out in the courtyard, with the foreigners gone. Sounds from the kitchen guided her.

Ghada placed al-Sadri outside the dining area with a pointed finger, where he could hide behind a large chair and watch the front door. The first boy she had sent off might return soon. Asher allowed himself to be guided to a spot to one side.

"I will approach and distract them," she murmured to the robot. "You remain here unless I need help."

She felt him nod and turned to the kitchen. At least one was washing dishes, but there were two voices chatting about horses and girls.

Boys.

Ghada slipped through the open door and peeked, memorizing this battlefield. One man elbows-deep in a sink basin. The other standing close by and smoking a cigarette. As she watched, he took it from his mouth and held it for the other man to take a drag.

She moved. Neither were looking her way.

A kick to the back of a knee was sufficient to flip the dishwasher over backwards, soapy water spraying everywhere as he did.

Ghada drove an elbow into the side of a skull on the other man, that same spot just behind the jaw where everything was sensitive. He dropped like a brick and bashed his forehead on the edge of the counter.

She turned to the first man and slapped an open palm into his groin with a painful sound.

He didn't even had time to whimper before he was also out.

She looked around and noted the weapons they had been holding, off to one side where they would remain dry. Just to cover her flank, she tossed them both into the sink with the dirty dishes. She could recover them later if she needed, and they would still fire for perhaps as much as a day.

"Asher," she said quietly as she watched.

The robot entered and gauged everything.

"I will carry these two to Zareen," he replied as he stepped close.

Ghada knew the man was stronger than human, but she still wasn't prepared for him to lift both like sacks of grain and walk out with them.

She emerged as well, following as far as the hallway where al-Sadri still kept watch. Now was when it would get tricky. She had no idea where the others might be, and any noise or shots fired would bring the remainder down on her.

Ghada supposed that she could take a weapon from her next victim and perhaps have al-Sadri carry it for now, but she needed to use her nudity offensively for as long as she could. Having a pistol in her hand would compromise that.

"Anything?" she asked as she stepped close to the Senussi warrior.

"No," he replied simply.

"How would you build a palace?" she turned to him.

He glanced over at her in thought, reddened, and went back to watching the front doors.

"I would place offices and a library down that hallway to the right," he said a moment later. "And a barracks for house servants to the left, beyond the kitchen."

"Let us try to eliminate the ones asleep, then," she said.

Asher rejoined them a few moments later and she moved out into the open. Again, nudity as a weapon, where the young men who saw her would not know how to react.

And everyone she had seen working here had been male.

She went down the empty hallway to a closed door and listened. Snoring. Barracks.

Ghada put the two men out of sight on either side and opened it.

Six men sleeping. Two more sitting at a table, one playing solitaire and the other reading a newspaper. The smoke from cigarettes was almost a physical manifestation in here.

No way to take them all silently.

Ghada smiled and walked towards the two at the table.

The one facing her glanced up, did a double-take, and muttered an obscenity under his breath.

Ghada kept the grin and continued walking.

The six were sleeping. She could see a rack and table off to one side where weapons were put without much thought, Hopefully, the safeties were on right now, but she didn't have particularly high expectations of her foes.

"What is this?" the man facing her growled.

The other man put down his newspaper and looked at her, flinching so hard he almost fell out of his chair. There was a rifle leaned against a wall nearby and a machine pistol on the table between the men, probably where one of them had laid it down when it banged against a chair back one time too many.

"Captain Bughra sent me," Ghada said provocatively in Tajik. "He didn't want you bored while he was gone, you know."

Ghada didn't think the man had more than glanced up at her face, let alone recognized her as one of his prisoners. Might have never seen an unclothed woman before in his life. Even rolls in the hay would probably involve just enough adjusting of clothing to do the deed.

He started to rise, but she gestured him to sit. The table was small enough for what she had in mind.

"You just sit for a bit and I'll put on a show for you," she cooed at the man, walking right up to him as he licked his lips in anticipation.

Ghada added an extra roll to her hips as she did, happy that men like that would prefer a bit more curves on a woman. Historians had described her figure as Rubenesque, especially compared to the Mistress, who had almost no curves or chest. Nudity just reinforced those extra bits, but no amount of exercise or training had done much to eliminate them.

But it certainly distracted these two men.

Ghada reached out her hands and put them on each man's shoulder. She needed to do this before they worked up the ambition to grope her in response, but they were just shepherds come down to town and still nervous around a pretty girl.

Ghada grabbed the backs of two heads and slammed them both into the surface of the table as hard as she could with surprise and leverage. One ended up cracking his forehead pretty solidly against the top of the other's head, so she lifted both and then slammed them down again, a little offset this time.

"Hey, what's going on?" a sleep-muddled voice asked.

Ghada turned and noted that one of the boys, possibly the youngest, had woken up and was turning upright to sit now. The other five wouldn't be too deep asleep.

She needed to move.

The distance was too great, and she didn't feel like being trapped in the middle of five or six of them if she made a mistake, so Ghada picked up the machine pistol, noting fresh blood from a broken nose on it, and pointed it at the lad.

"If you remain perfectly silent, I won't kill you," she said with a smile.

"Is this a joke?" he asked, staring at a naked woman pointing a gun at him.

"No," Ghada replied. "Emad, Asher, could you join me and close the door?"

The boy stared at her, still fascinated but extremely confused.

He flinched a little when the others entered, but didn't provoke her.

"How many more men on the grounds?" Ghada asked, stepping close enough to keep his eyes focused on her and his mind utterly confused.

"Three," he answered blankly, still obviously trying to find a spot in his universe that included a naked woman with a machine pistol.

Emad and Asher woke the others quietly, guns pointed as the men rose. She had accounted for an even dozen now. Three meant that there were a half dozen that had left, presumably at the airstrip where Finn and Hans had gone off with Captain Bughra to provide this opening.

She hadn't expected to be this successful, but she had caught them off-guard. No shooting meant that she might actually be able to control the situation, at least until the first boy returned with a doctor for a non-existent medical emergency. But that meant that someone would be able to set broken noses and deal with concussions adequately.

Asher set to work ripping blankets and tying hands and feet. It would keep the men controlled, which was good.

Ghada would feel bad if she had to kill all these boys, but that wouldn't stop her if it became necessary. The Mistress hadn't known all the things she'd done over the last several years when certain individuals became a little too forward or interested in their activities.

Quickly, the eight in here were disabled. Asher and Emad

raced off then to get the others, leaving her with these prisoners to watch. Ghada enjoyed the way they mixed lust, confusion, and embarrassment.

A moment later, the door opened. Far too soon for the men to arrive.

A pair of men walked in, chatting about something, with the first looking back over his shoulder at the one trailing.

He entered and stopped dead when Ghada rose from where she'd been sitting on an empty bed and pointed the gun at him.

"Good morning," she said. "If you move, I will kill you both."

Simple. Clear. Deadly.

The second man moved around the first to see what the problem was, and froze as well.

Naked woman as Death.

Ghada wondered if she could commission an artist to immortalize her thus.

"Drop your guns on the bed, right now," Ghada ordered in a rising voice.

Possibly the one their mothers used when they misbehaved. Farm boys, after all. They reacted the same. Guns came off shoulders when the boys realized that eight of their companions had already apparently fallen to a single woman.

Death, as a nude, smiling.

"Move over there," she pointed, getting them out of the way of the door.

They goggled, but complied. Seeing all of your friends tied up and gagged would certainly lend credence. And nobody really woke up on any given morning expecting to be killed.

"Sit down, with your hands on your knees," Ghada continued, stepping around beds to keep everyone in view.

Again, compliance.

Ghada would never admit to how much fun she was having right now, but she also wouldn't deny it. Foolish boys and their masculine expectations of authority, and all that.

The door opened a few moments later, drawing her barrel, but it was the Mistress, leading a convoy of more bound and confused prisoners. Those got added to the mix. If the first lad had been telling the truth, there was only one left, probably in an office off the other wing, and the one that had gone for help.

"Mistress, you and Emad cover these," Ghada ordered. "Asher and I will collect the last two strays for you."

"Deal," Zareen smiled and nodded, before turning her own face into a harridan and scowling at the men lining the walls. Asher tied the last two and then she went back out into the hallway.

"Asher, you hold this for me, but I do not require you to even point it at someone, let alone shoot them," Ghada said.

"Thank you." He took it by the barrel and followed her back to the big foyer. "I have studied human cultures for more than two decades, but this is not a tactic I have encountered before, Ghada. Why did it work?"

"They are just boys, Asher," she murmured. "They have never seen a woman nude before, most likely, but had dreamed of such a thing. They would be confused by lust, but I can defeat any two of them in unarmed combat easily. Surprise works wonders in such situations."

"That much is obvious," he agreed.

She started down the other hallway and noted a light on as she approached. With a gesture, she set Asher against a side wall, looking back to cover the entry, as she walked right up to the door and entered.

The man behind the desk was older. This looked like the team's accountant, but still not a sergeant capable of commanding in Bughra's absence. He looked up at her and his jaw fell open.

Ghada walked to the side of the desk and smiled. If he had a pistol, it was either in a holster where he couldn't get to it quickly, or in a drawer.

"You are my prisoner," Ghada announced quietly. "I have

already captured the rest of your men. If you provoke me right now, I will hurt you, so you should surrender."

His eyes had gone glassy, but it was shock, not lust. Well, tinged a little with lust, which brightened her morning. Too many men saw the beautiful face of the Mistress and ignored the maid.

Nobody was ignoring her today.

"All of them?" he finally gasped.

"I have fourteen men tied up already," Ghada replied with a grin. "You make fifteen, assuming I don't have to kill you right now. The boy I sent to town for a doctor will be the last. Do you wish to surrender or die?"

"But how?" he asked blankly.

Ghada just smiled.

"Fine," he said, beginning to rise. "I am your prisoner."

He was lying. The man practically announced it with the way he stood and how his hands moved.

Ghada let him lash out at her then moved her hand and head just enough that the punch missed. Because she had given him the option, she struck him in the belly now, hard enough to fold him in half. And then grabbed the back of his head and slammed his face into the desk. Not enough to kill him, but more than enough to concuss his brain.

Then she took his closer hand and twisted it up and behind in such a way that he had to do what she wanted if he didn't want to lose his arm entirely. Not even surgery would fix it, if she started tearing things right now.

He settled and she drove the man forward, back into the hall where Asher watched both directions with his acute hearing.

"It did not appear that you needed assistance," Asher observed.

That was another reason she liked the robot. He didn't assume women were a lesser gender that needed to be protected all the time. Finn and Emad meant well, but they were products of their era and culture.

Ghada nodded and walked her prisoner forward, *blasé* about her current nudity. They got to the big foyer and the front door opened.

She looked over and the first boy was leading an older man with the requisite black, leather bag into the palace. They both froze when they saw her and her prisoner.

"It was a ruse to get you off the premises," Ghada said. "But if you surrender right now, I won't leave you in a condition of needing a doctor."

Blank, glassy-eyed looks, both of them.

"What the young lady is saying is that we don't want to have to kill you, but will," Asher announced, going so far as to point her gun at the men.

Neither of the newer two were armed. Hands went up, one still holding the bag.

"Follow me," Ghada ordered, confident that Asher would handle them if necessary.

She got back to the barracks and added to her menagerie of farm boys.

"What have you done?" the doctor demanded.

"Concussions and broken noses for the most part," Ghada replied. "Everyone was compliant enough that I didn't have to shoot them. If you promise to behave, I'll allow you to treat the worst injured."

More shock, but Ghada just kept her smile.

"You should probably get dressed now," Zareen said, pointing to a pile of clothes.

Ghada shrugged. She'd made her point today. The men had been given an understanding that she was more than just Zareen's maid. The farm boys would approach any naked woman with a great deal more care and nervousness in the future.

Now she just had to go rescue Finn and Hans.

CHAPTER TWENTY-FOUR

Finn didn't like the way the Condor handled with the bombs on the wings, but Hans had warned him. Rode heavy, like a tired horse on that last homeward stretch before it could smell the bucket of oats in the barn.

Hans was still up front, at least providing a sun shade this morning. Bughra was behind him, hopefully falling into that dozing state that civilians suffered from when they first flew, with the noise and vibration lulling them to sleep.

"There is your turn," Hans called, pointing to a spot on the right. "The road to the pass."

Finn banked her over softly and lined himself up with the road going out of town to the general southeast. He could see the mountains in the distance where the road curved around behind, following the road up into where it turned and crossed into China at Erkeshtam Pass.

He couldn't see it from here, but the map had showed the deep gorge where the southern flank of the Tian Shan Mountains met the Pamir Mountains. Still, he had elevation, so Finn also started pushing for altitude, just to see what his actual flight ceiling might be today.

Hans had been a little full of shit about not being able to

make it over these mountains, because he had a normal top of sixty-five hundred meters, at least according to the documentation he read. But Finn also knew that age, maintenance, and weather factored heavily on things. Plus dragging along a couple of big bombs underneath him that messed with his flight envelope.

"We can make it, yes?" Bughra yelled over the sound of the engines.

Finn glanced back.

"We can, but it's not as simple as just pointing at a direction on the horizon," Finn replied. "Winds get strange over the mountains and passes, so I plan to fly over the actual pass, rather than trying to work my way straight. Plus, I have to fly this by sight, since there are no radio beacons around here I would trust to keep my heading."

"Complicated, I understand," Bughra said. "But we will strike a serious blow against the Nationalists and perhaps today avenge the East Turkestan Republic that those damned Hui destroyed in 1934."

Finn shrugged and focused on the way the wind patterns got messy around him. These mountains were all sharp with twisting canyons, so it was almost like riding a raft through whitewater to keep things in control.

Hopefully, there wasn't anybody down there with a telescope and a radio, calling back his description to someone with big enough guns to knock him and the Condor out of the sky. Aircraft was already going to be a new enough thing that people would be watching. He didn't need to get his ass shot down on top of it. Hadn't even gotten out the parachutes today, but he almost never did, except to check and make sure they were still packed right and no mice had nibbled on them.

Finn glanced back now and studied the man, keeping things level and straight with his hands.

"So I assume you're going to drop the bombs, Captain," he said loud enough to be heard over the hum of the engines. He waited for the man to nod before continuing. "In that case, this is where it gets a little complicated at our end."

"How so?" Bughra demanded.

"The bombardier lays on the floor where Hans is sitting right now," Finn told the man. "There's a bomb sight he uses to identify his target, based on elevation and speed. I'll still be flying, but you two will need to trade places at some point."

Finn turned his head forward again, ignoring the man. Hans was doing the same.

Wasn't Finn's fault nobody had asked earlier how it was done. And he was already going to be committing enough crimes today. Finn didn't need that on his rap sheet, too.

Finn imagined he could hear Bughra chewing nails back there, but there were no two ways about it. Finn had to fly. Bughra wouldn't want to rely on Hans dropping the bombs at the right instant to actually damage anything, instead of just scaring some camels or something. He'd have to get down on his belly to do the deed.

And then Finn would teach him a few things about flying.

But best to let the fellow work himself up to it slowly, ya know?

"How soon?" Bughra demanded.

Finn shrugged.

"Couple of hours yet," he called back to the man, turning enough to just glance. "We're cruising at about three hundred kph right now, but we've got some winding and maneuvering to do to get where we want to be to line things up on Kashgar. I presume you'll know what an army base looks like from the air and direct me when we get everything in sight on the other side of the mountains."

More silence. Man had had himself a bright idea to hijack a plane and strap some bombs on, but never really thought about things at the sharp end of the spear. Finn had never flown combat, being in a spotter plane for the artillery during the ruckus, and then at a point where most of the dangerous

German pilots were dead and they were sending kids up to get splattered by folks like Eddie Rickenbacker and others.

Hell, he could have told Bughra what an army base looked like from up here. Seen and flown over enough of them in his time, both as a soldier and a civilian. Might even, if the man asked nice enough, assuming things hadn't changed once they were over China.

"Fertig, if we do trade places, is there a way I can put you in the rear of the aircraft and lock the door?" Bughra finally called, once he'd had time to sort it out in his head.

Hell of a complicated choreography, an aircraft this small. Not a lot of places for three bodies to move around each other, especially when one of them was holding the draw on the other two. Finn didn't have a gun, but he was more than willing to bet on the big Kraut. Probably a couple of spare sausages and four or five bottles of hooch as well.

You never knew with Hans.

"*Ja,*" Hans turned now and called. "You can jam something in the latch from this side. Plus, the aircraft sounds different with it open. Step back and try it."

Hans didn't move, but he had no place to maneuver to if the man took it in his head to start shooting. The glass around them should stop bullets, but that just meant that they would bounce all over the damned place before they stopped. Finn had a plate of armor right behind his seat, but that only covered his heart and kidneys against shots from chasing planes. Easy enough for Bughra to step to his right.

"When we get over the pass, you and I will trade places, Fertig," Bughra called. "You can remain in back until we are done and returning home."

"As you wish," Hans called in a bored voice that just told Finn where he had stashed a gun for himself.

Somewhere aft. Maybe he'd have Hans show him, just in case someone else decided to shanghai them one of these days.

Outside, the Condor was coming around a curve in the

mountains that let him see where the road climbed out onto the plateau at the top of the world. Beautiful country around here, for all that it was kind of a desert. There were glaciers in several places that reminded him of Switzerland, and that brought him a kind of peace.

Things were going to get a little ugly on the other side of the pass.

CHAPTER TWENTY-FIVE

Didier had moved to a seat where he could look out a window and watch the ground sweep by beneath them. And it moved him away from the Fraulein and her overt sexuality.

Didier still wondered if she would knock at his door this evening to make demands. Konrad didn't look like a man that might keep up with her, being more dry and scholarly. She had shown no interest in Bertrand, which was a shame, because he was the same sort of predator as she was.

A match made in hell, if he'd ever seen one.

So he kept his distance and made his plans in silence, even as Konrad and Reiher sat on the comfortable benches and read.

Didier had never been this deep into Asia. No reason, as the Soviets had closed all their frontiers after winning their Civil War against the western nations that had been allies of the Tsar before Lenin took power from Kerensky.

Not even to visit Tunguska, after he had learned about the place and the event. Was that where the Man With No Face was taking them? Deep into the Siberian wilderness?

On the one hand, it would be the perfect place to drag off all the witnesses and kill them quietly. Or even not so quietly, with nothing but trees for thousands of kilometers in every direction.

In that, he would not necessarily mind catching up with them, if he could find a way to feed these obnoxious Germans into the alien's maw first and still somehow escape himself.

Or was this a sign from some higher or alien power that he should abandon the chase entirely? Pursuing the Man With No Face alone was a useful thing, but what if he had true alien allies that might wish to retain their secrecy? Would they kill him as well, just to protect themselves?

There was no easy answer, so he moved back to where Bertrand sat and planted himself close across the aisle.

"Trouble?" the assassin asked.

"We move further and further into the unknown, Bertrand," Didier replied grimly. "In Lisbon, it might have been a simple parlor game to pursue these secrets, following Shirazi around and trying to swoop in on her at the end."

"Not anymore?" Bertrand turned to look at him.

"The game grows larger," Didier shrugged. "Germany takes note. I cannot imagine that even the fools in the French government will miss this parade of aircraft and questions and therefore decide that they need to send their own spies to bother us. Or worse, to try to inveigle us into upholding them against the Germans and the British."

"We need to kill everyone and disappear again?" the man asked as he smiled.

"You should be prepared for it, yes," Didier decided. "But not at Samarkand. They will have flown again, possibly only be a half-day ahead of us now, and the German pilot will not take orders from me. Nor will the various embassies and spies that Konrad has engaged to assist him."

Bertrand studied his face. Didier felt more tired than anything else.

"But yes," he continued. "If we are headed to Tunguska, then you and I probably need to, at the minimum, arrange to be left behind. Let Shirazi and the Man With No Face kill them for us. We will find another way after them later, assuming the aliens have not killed Shirazi as well."

Even a killer like Bertrand blanched at that, but he was a professional assassin. There had been several times he could have killed the woman, but Didier had never ordered it. Didier appreciated that, as she had made an effective hound, tracking down clues and information for him.

But this might be endgame now, and only a fool rushed in.

Bertrand nodded grimly. Didier did not miss Fraulein Reiher glancing up and smiling at him, as if she could read his mind.

Was she also preparing a double-cross? He suspected that the Germans would keep him on a leash and follow, only to deny him his victory in the end. After all, Germany had long seen France as a greater enemy than the Slavs. Hitler had not changed that much, other than he might capture France in the next war and use all that wealth to finance a crusade that eliminated Russia entirely and extended the Reich to the Pacific.

Didier would die before he would allow that.

Perhaps the first shots would be exchanged at Samarkand.

CHAPTER TWENTY-SIX

Zareen smiled at her prisoners. Asher and Emad had tied them all sufficiently now that none could escape in the short term. At the same time, none was at risk of losing limbs from blood loss.

Emad was watching the front, since he looked the most like the others, lacking a beard but at least being male. Asher carried a gun, but would not use it. That left her and Ghada, standing well away from the men where they could talk.

"Separating the party is dangerous," Ghada agreed. "Finn and Hans will presumably return in a few hours. Do we shoot out the tires of most of the vehicles and tear out the telephone wire?"

"That would immobilize them," Zareen nodded. "We probably can't find all of their weapons, but enough that they would not wish to attack us, were we to move to the airstrip to ambush Bughra when he returns."

"Will Finn and Hans have already handled that?" Ghada asked.

Zareen paused rather than immediately reply. That was entirely possible. In fact, they might be in a position to simply refuel the Condor and take off again as fast as the machinery would fill the tanks.

Where could they go from here? That would depend entirely on luck.

If Finn had bombed Kashgar, then they would need to flee west and south now. Possibly back to Tehran and then her home precincts. Sell the Condor and replace it like they had done *Cerberus* when that aircraft became too notorious. Only then would they be able to consider the Tibetan Plateau and a place that might yet be a hidden Durren base, abandoned but presumably secured before they left.

Zareen looked up. The men were still in a state of shock, despite Ghada being dressed now for adventure, abandoning even the pretense of being demure. Her outfit looked remarkably like Zareen's in that, cut in the same manner but fitting a woman with more curves. Jodhpurs, white shirt, tweed vest, and even a gun belt for a pistol that she was not wearing, with the machine pistol instead.

"Asher," Zareen whispered as if still talking to Ghada. "Nod if you are listening to what I'm saying, but otherwise do not react."

His head bobbed once.

"I will continue guarding the men in here," Zareen continued ever so quietly. "Ghada will watch the front where Emad is now, while Asher will take Emad and begin disabling all of the vehicles except one, however you see fit to do so. Locate a telephone wire and cut it such that it cannot be easily repaired, and check the office for any radio with range sufficient to contact an aircraft or even the airstrip."

She looked at Ghada and got a nod. Those two immediately left and Zareen studied the men that Ghada had called farmboys.

"It is my intention to depart shortly," Zareen announced in Tajik. "You have been polite enough that we will simply leave you here after we disable your automobiles, and Captain Bughra can untie you when he returns. Stay away from the airstrip. In fact, do not leave this compound before noon tomorrow, because if I do encounter any of you in town, where me and my party might have to spend the night before we continued on our journey, I will just kill you all as soon as I see you. Am I clear?"

She pointedly looked at each man in sequence until he nodded back at her.

They might not believe her, but they had all also been captured by a naked, unarmed woman, so they would have their reservations about causing her trouble. Captain Bughra might convince them otherwise, but he would likely doubt their stories about what Ghada had done to them.

Zareen could have warned the man. But that would have spoiled her surprise. And her fun.

Hopefully, Finn and Hans had survived their encounter with the man, and everyone could reset to a clean slate tomorrow.

She would, certainly, not cross through Samarkand again, anytime soon. At least not without bringing several of Ghada's younger sisters or nieces with her. That might be its own revolution in Uzbekistan, but the Soviets were supposedly all about equality of the sexes, as little as they seemed to actually honor it with positions of power.

After Persia returned to the world stage, kicking out the Russians and the British, she might have a long and frank conversation with them about that. Or she might just destroy their armies and put a new Catherine the Great on the Tsar's throne and let the woman kick the men into the Twentieth Century.

She smiled at the boys around her, most of them her age or perhaps even older, but so much less sophisticated. All of them withered and paled under that gaze, which was her intent.

A few minutes passed and Ghada came to the door.

"It is done," she said simply as she surveyed things and smiled her own pretty smile at the boys.

They flinched even more.

"Goodbye," Zareen said as she moved to the door. "And good luck on a long life where I don't have to kill all of you."

And then she was out the door, pulling it shut and locking it from this side. The men inside would be furiously straining and twisting now, but Asher had assured her that they would struggle in vain for some time before succeeding.

Still, she raced to the front door on Ghada's heels. The men had kept an old Ford flatbed truck in working shape. Ghada climbed up into the bed with Asher, gesturing her to climb into the cab where Emad drove. Zareen noted a box of machine pistols and rifles in the bed with Asher, so presumably the compound was largely disarmed at present.

There would be men at the airport just as heavily armed, so it would be necessary to sneak up and scout that situation as well. Hopefully, they would be no more focused on their duties than the farm boys had been, and Zareen's party could get the drop on them.

But she was not above starting a small shooting war over possession of the airstrip.

The bandits in this town needed to learn that there were worse predators than them lurking about.

CHAPTER TWENTY-SEVEN

Finn was amazed by the gorge as he flew over Erkeshtam Pass. Notes he'd encountered on various maps marked this as the western edge of China historically. The folks behind him had been agitating for a Turkmen nation on the far side, but the locals over there, Uighur or Hui or whoever they were, had forced the Turkmen out a few years ago, siding with the Han Chinese in the process. At least if he understood the story correctly.

Apparently they'd killed Bughra's favorite cousin and a few others at the same time. Had he known just how crazy it had gotten up here, Finn figured he'd have fought harder to convince Zareen and Asher to circle in counter-clockwise from the Chungking side. Or maybe come over Nepal or something from British India. China's Civil War was a mess, but he'd never intended to fly through a second one where the Russians were maybe trying to slice themselves off control of those passes into China.

The old Great Game that never seemed to go away.

"Okay, Bughra, we're now officially in China," Finn called over his shoulder, wondering if the man was asleep, he'd been so quiet for the last hour.

They had pretty good altitude, but Finn was looking forward to losing the bombs. No way in hell he'd make it back to Samarkand with that much drag. Better to stop in Osh or someplace and refuel, but then he'd have to explain things to a whole different set of officials that he didn't figure Bughra had bribed yet.

Or had the local Soviet been issuing orders? He wasn't sure how much the good Captain was a bandit hanging out in the city versus a spy for the local government, maybe one that provided the Soviets a convenient excuse when someone dropped bombs on a Chinese army.

According to Bughra, when he wasn't a little frothy at the mouth, there had been a government of East Turkestan before 1934, but the survivors had officially called it off and joined with some other army.

Not his problem.

"Fertig, you will please move to the rear with me, so that we can change places," Bughra ordered.

At least he said please. That might matter with the big Kraut later.

Finn heard the hatch open behind him, upping the sound significantly. Hans hadn't been lying about that part.

Hans unbuckled and turned to face the rear, his face a mask so bland that Finn figured the man had just drawn an inside straight. As long as nobody opened fire inside here, Finn would be fine.

He concentrated on the horizon. The road below was a little twisty here as it followed the valley, but Kashgar itself was almost a straight shot due east, a little over one hundred and eighty kilometers away. Twenty minutes or so if he opened the throttles wide, but that would eat up too much fuel that way, so he just kept things steady.

Nothing stupid happened aft, which was good. Finn heard the hatch close and assumed that Bughra was putting something in the latch to hold it shut. Wouldn't work, but he wasn't going to tell the man that.

Captain Bughra slipped around him, keeping the pistol on his far side, obviously expecting Finn to do something stupid right now. Finn just looked at him like a cow with a particularly good cud.

Man got past and sat sideways on the forward seat, trying to look at the bombsight at the same time he watched Finn.

"So you end up face down on the deck, right about where you would be to operate the machine gun," Finn called over the noise. "Bombsight is still there, even though they took out the bay when they built it into a passenger carrier for me. As you found, the hooks on the wings for external racks were still there as was the wiring."

"Does it work?" Bughra called back.

"Got no clue," Finn answered. "You were the one working on it with Hans, remember? I was just a civilian off to one side with two minders. Hans thought it would or he'd have never sent us up here with them. You tell me what altitude you want to fly over and I hold it as steady as I can. You dial it in on the doohickey and then as soon as you drop them I turn us on one wing and run like hell in case there are any interceptors around here that might chase us. You and Hans will haul your asses aft in that case and man the various machine guns if that happens. Am I clear?"

He might have gotten a little hot by the end of that, but he really hadn't thought about having to outrun other aircraft up here. Assuming he could. All the guns were loaded and worked, just because Hans had them and had the ammunition.

Finn watched the man process all that diatribe in one swoop. Wasn't like he'd gotten the rough edge of Finn's tongue before now. Hopefully, wouldn't have to again later, but Finn reserved the right at the moment.

"What is a safe height?" Bughra asked now.

Finn didn't roll his eyes at the guy. Man was asking, as

opposed to assuming he had all the answers. Still a kidnapper, but not being as asshole about things. Not like Muskegon.

"One thousand meters is a nice, round number," Finn yelled. "Gives me some flexibility to maneuver and keeps us low enough that everything is clear. No clouds or rain today, so much easier to do this."

"Would you have tried this in the rain?" Bughra turned and looked at him.

"Would I have had a choice in the matter, had the forecast said storms?" Finn fired back.

Bughra flinched a little under the tone. Man was reconsidering that maybe he didn't know everything there was to know. That might be a useful thing, as it meant the punk had the capacity to grow up and act like a responsible adult, instead of a bandit down from the mountains.

"You do not care, one way or the other, do you?" Bughra asked, turned fully this way now, sideways on the forward seat.

Finn checked his elevation against the tendency of the nose to drift lower. Still steady and smooth. Not following the road, but trying to center on the gorge itself, where a little bit of a tailwind was pushing and saving him fuel. He pulled back a shade, gaining some height even as the ground slowly started to fade away below them.

"I got hired by Shirazi to fly," Finn answered. Wasn't even an evasion, so much as lie by omission. "Will keep doing that after you and I are done doing this stupid stunt."

"Stupid?" Bughra's face grew angry.

"Stupid," Finn repeated. "We've got a pair of bombs. Big deal. I drop them on someplace interesting. Let's say maybe you score a hit. What does it matter, unless you happen to kill someone important? They'll bring in another general. World's full of them, or colonels jealous enough to want a promotion. Won't destroy an army. Won't even damage it all that much, except for the fellows you manage to kill. Next time you want to try a stunt like this, they'll have cannon in place, pointing at the sky, and blow one lone bomber out of the sky. Even if you come in at night, which would be suicidal with all this wind and the mountains around us. Ain't nothing going to change."

"They killed my cousin," Bughra growled at him, possibly getting to the heart of the matter.

"Understood," Finn said. "But you'd need a whole army backing you up, and maybe an air corps as well, if you want to actually push those silly bastards back out of the desert. Personally, I think you're better off finding more planes and troops, if you want to try it, but you didn't hire me for my combat experience. Just to fly you around."

"You were a soldier?" Bughra blinked in surprise. "Where?"

"France in the Great War, son," Finn snapped. Man really wasn't more than a kid, for all he was in charge of that mob back in town. Russia had been at war since 1914 with the rest of them, but theirs didn't end in '18 when Finn went home. As much home as he had before he came back to France, anyway. Bughra had probably been weaned on fighting, except that it never got that interesting down south here, whatever the Turkmen and Hui did in Kashgar notwithstanding. "Started as a rifleman. Managed to get myself promoted to pilot. Been flying since 1918."

"Could you build an air army to help us push the Chinese back?" Bughra asked, all solicitous now.

Finn shrugged and watched the horizon on his gauges. Still a little high, climbing out of the gorge.

"You'd need Stalin and the folks in Moscow funding you to get anything done," Finn replied. "Don't remember hearing about them wanting to do much. Hell, they're barely fighting the Japanese in the Far East in Manchuria. Don't see them invading China from this end. Not without a good reason."

The man stewed for a long minute. Finn figured he finally had his elevation about where he wanted it and smiled at the fellow.

"You should probably get ready," Finn said. "I got no idea what I'm aiming for, and Kashgar is coming up pretty quickly."

Bughra nodded, still grumpy, and slipped his pistol into the holster, closing the flap and securing it. He stood and turned, looking at the space he would need to slide into.

Finn slammed the Condor into a dive.

He hoped the big Kraut had been smart enough to strap himself in back there, so he didn't bounce his head off the ceiling like Bughra just did. Sounded a mite painful.

Just to be sure, Finn rolled onto his right wing and flattened out a little, this time bouncing the Russian off the side window and then the chair where he'd just been sitting.

Now, the impressive bit. Finn rolled flat and put the plane into a 9.8 dive. Falling at the speed of gravity. Great trick to pick up an empty can of beer like it was flying and drop it into a trashcan behind you.

Or a Russian bandit.

Bughra levitated slowly backwards until he was even with Finn.

Finn pulled up abruptly and slammed the guy into the deck now, setting the autopilot with one hand as he reached down and punched the man as hard as he could without unstrapping first.

"HANS!" he yelled, but the hatch behind him was already open and the big Kraut came in behind a teeny pistol.

Just because Hans was like that, he punched the man as well, dropping all that Teutonic weight on the Russian as he did.

"Dead or alive?" Hans asked, looking up.

"Tie him up for now," Finn replied. "I need to find a quiet place to scare some mountain goats so I can get all this damned weight off my wings."

Hans disarmed the man and grabbed him, dragging the limp figure out of sight as Finn studied the horizon on his left.

Best bet at this point was to just find a spot where he could cross the mountains. Like a pigeon, he knew exactly where he was in relation to both Kashgar and Osh, so he could cross now and come out in a pretty good spot.

The California Condor agreed as he rolled over on his left wing and started climbing again. Pilot had a lever where he could drop the wing bombs, in addition to the bombardier. Hans had added it when he built the rest, although Finn had no clue why at the time.

Understood now and it saved him from Hans having to leave Bughra alone in back while someone dropped those ugly, black eggs on a Chinese mountain.

Pretty quick, Finn was alone with his thoughts. No villages up this high that he could see, but he also wanted to be on the other side, so he held off until the Condor crossed over.

He could almost smell the line across the ridge of the mountains when they crossed back into Russia. Finn studied the terrain and turned to the west, running along the first, highest valley, if you could call it that. Good enough.

"HANS, HANG ON!" Finn yelled.

He counted to five and released the bombs.

Condor was far happier without the weight, soaring suddenly as Finn rolled away to the north.

Behind them, a pair of bombs went boom and set off all manner of avalanches, but Finn hadn't seen anyone that would get hurt, so he came out ahead.

Finn sniffed the air and pointed his nose at Osh, first step on the path back to Samarkand.

Then he'd have to deal with everybody else.

CHAPTER TWENTY-EIGHT

Emad drove the Ford hard. He had stolen it after all, just like a nearly identical model back in the Cyrenaican desert, and wasn't going to be keeping it for long, so using it up right now was fine.

He remembered the airstrip from yesterday. Had it only been yesterday?

A single strip out on the edge of town, flattened by heavy equipment, with a small aerodrome at one end, but not much traffic. Tehran had actually been as busy as Cairo, but this reminded him more of Acre. That would still work to their advantage, especially if Bughra's men recognized the vehicle and let him get close enough that they could be captured.

The truck came over a rise and Emad jammed the clutch down hard and rolled off to the side of the barely marked road.

"What is it?" Zareen asked sharply.

He killed the engine and pointed to the aircraft he saw in the distance.

"That is not the California Condor," Emad said. "But it is a very similar Heinkel H-111."

They could be quite certain that it was not the aircraft he

sought. This one had the tail fin painted bright red, with a white circle in the center and black swastika.

"What are the odds that this is a random chance meeting?" Zareen asked after a moment.

"Very low, actually," Asher said, loud enough to be heard in the open window. "There is a car loading right now. I recognize Didier Beauchêne as one of the three people getting into the back, and the assassin Bertrand standing with a separate group to ride into town, presumably the flight crew."

"So they have been following us?" Zareen asked.

"It would seem so," Emad noted. "If the Frenchman is with them, one would presume that they were in the vicinity of Cairo while we were farther east. Perhaps they had spies that tracked us to Acre, and have been notifying their network to follow us. But we need to turn around and vanish immediately."

"Agreed," Zareen said. "This is the main road to town and they might recognize us, or at least note that something is wrong with this truck."

Emad pressed the clutch in and then the starter, listening to the engine turn over roughly before it caught. Now was not the time for it to die by the side of the road, just as their enemies were coming.

He got it into gear with a grind and managed to turn around.

"They are heading to town?" he yelled over the sound of the engine and road. "Do we presume that they have not yet heard the news? Have not realized that Finn and Hans are due back soon?"

"It is a risk we will have to take," she said before raising her voice. "Asher, you and Ghada keep watch both ways for all of our various enemies."

Emad concentrated on driving, getting back to a fork that would take them right back to the compound if they continued down it, but different from the one the Frenchman would take with his allies to get to town.

He wondered if that group would end up staying at the very same hotel that Zareen had originally selected, before Captain Bughra and his band had snuck up on them. Emad and Ghada had discussed operational security for Zareen before now. He was willing to let the other woman drive that conversation, mostly because he was an outsider there. At the same time, he had seen those dance moves she practiced on a daily basis and finally understood what they were really for.

And she had several other women from her clan similarly trained? As an Arab man, he found it hard to wrap his head around a culture that not only allowed women such training, but insisted on it. And like Ghada Attar, more such women could easily be invisible warriors in the eyes of men like Emad had once been.

He smiled.

"What is so funny?" Zareen asked as they came around a small curve, out of sight, and Emad slowed to a halt. There was a wide spot here that he could use to turn around without having to back more than once.

"Ghada's sister and cousins, like some band of deadly, Sufi mystics coming out of the night." Emad turned to smile at the woman next to him as he rotated the wheel.

"You are closer to the truth than you probably realize, Emad al-Sadri," she said in a serious tone, casting a chilling pall on his soul as the implications became clear. "Persia is nominally Shia, unlike the lands south of the Euphrates, but her village verges over onto apostasy that way. There have been more than one famous Sufi scholar and wanderer from her valley. Those lands fall within my family's ancestral territory, so they have served my family for more generations than you might believe. My mother sending Ghada with me on this adventure was not a lightly taken decision."

"And we will return for more such guardians?" Emad asked carefully.

"It is probably necessary at this point," she shrugged. "But not immediately. For now, we will go to the place Asher has found and see what mysteries the Durren might have left us."

"What if there is a radio by which we might contact them?" he asked as he eased off the clutch and started to bring the truck around again.

Ford build durable vehicles, but they were not always pleasant to drive. Still better than the armored car he and his men had stolen from the Italians, though.

"I am not sure what I would do, Emad," Zareen replied. "On the one hand, they might help us with the technology to usher in a new Golden Age on Earth. At the same time, they would likely see Asher as a criminal to be imprisoned and destroyed for what the others did. Plus, if the Germans have allied with our French foe, they would use such technology badly, in pursuit of their mad dreams of world conquest."

"So we might lead them astray instead?" Emad asked as he got the beast turned around and left it pulled to the side of the road. He went ahead and killed it again for now. The other party would require some time to go past in the distance, down across the low valley.

"We are not nearly socially advanced enough to perhaps master such things, Emad," she offered into the sudden stillness.

Only the breeze made a sound, other than his heartbeat.

Emad studied the woman.

Like him, an outsider growing up, a child of two cultures, barely accepted by either. In both of their cases at least one parent of noble blood, such as it was measured these days. Raised in two cultures in her case, although Emad supposed that he was raised both for the palace and the saddle, so he also shared that with her.

Neither had broached the topic that sat between them on

the bench seat right now. He understood why. And now was not the time, either, but he could see that in her eyes as well.

"So when do you think we will advance far enough to join some interstellar society?" Emad asked.

He had borrowed a few of Hans Fertig's strange scientifiction books, mostly to practice his English the same way the German man did. But it also let him think about such things as life on other worlds, however strange such denizens might be.

"The League of Nations was a good step, but it failed because of the obstinacy of the Americans," she said quietly. "Similarly, there were many treaties signed in the last twenty years that would have set us on a better path, but the rising fascist nations, as well as Imperial Japan, seem intent on casting them aside and returning to a harsher reality, such as what Britain emerged from a century ago. I fear it will be done in fits and starts, but no real progress will be made while men like Hitler and Mussolini continue to push the bounds of acceptable behavior."

"Is that why you resist them, Zareen?" he asked, letting the conversation stay on grand political topics instead.

"The world will never rise above its current state while we continue to maintain empires," she replied. "While the British meddle in the Near East for their own purposes, setting everyone against the other. The same with the Russians. In the Pacific, the Americans seem intent on doing the same."

"So Egypt and Libya should be free?" Emad asked, drifting back to the places dearest to his heart.

"I am not that convinced even in the concept of Libya, Emad," she said, turning more to face him. "Would not Cyrenaica as a separate thing from both Fezzan and Tripoli, as has historically been the case, be a better outcome, as the cultures are so different?"

"And Persia?" Emad asked, pushing back a little now.

She grimaced, but he could see the same fire in her eyes.

"The Russians stripped off the Caucasus from our old lands

a century ago," she nodded. "Many folks abandoned their lands when the Russians moved in and claimed them, while at the same time many Armenians left Persia for the north. In that, you have seen cultures centering better on themselves, so just ending the rule of the Qajars with a less corrupt government would go a long ways. Plus, the Russians will eventually need to be broken, to the point that all of their imperial subjects could be freed to their own self-determination. But I must defeat the Italians in Africa and the Germans in Europe first. Does that make sense?"

He nodded. As far as Emad could tell, she had never been so explicit with outsiders, although Ghada might have already known this. That she was telling him indicated a level of greater trust.

Emad al-Sadri could build on that. They were both outsiders of good families. He would never inherit any great authority from Idris or his own cousins, so if life took him permanently into Persia, they would not find it a great loss, other than he would be living among Shia. Or perhaps Sufi, depending. His Sunni soul found that acceptable.

"It does," he answered her obvious question, as well as some of the lower layers.

Such as: Would he be willing to help her fight a war against the British and Russians after they finished with the fascists?

Emad had not been so sure, even an hour ago, but the arrival of a swastika in Soviet Central Asia had broken something loose in his soul. Those men would not be satisfied with anything less than total domination of the world.

Idly, he wondered if the Nazis could be convinced to attack the Russians at some point, thinking Stalin a pushover. Napoleon had been so inclined, and it had not worked out for him a century and a half ago.

Emad had read extensively on Bonaparte and his eventual destroyer, Wellington. The Peninsular Campaign had invented the term *guerrilla* to describe civilians slipping in and out of a little war to resist an occupying force. More recently, the Italians had been lousy soldiers but excellent instructors.

They waited in silence while he considered all the ways that his personal war in Cyrenaica might turn into a world-wide conflagration. All the kindling was packed and dry, awaiting only the spark.

Was he seated next to the woman who would ignite it?

He glanced over and smiled at her, caught her smiling at him.

Without the war and clandestine intrigue around her, he would be courting the woman right now. Flowers and poetry inspired by Gibran. Tea under the watchful eye of Ghada Attar, who was far more dangerous than *anybody else* had given her credit for before today.

Would there ever be space for such a thing in Zareen's life? Emad was not sure. He had been raised in a culture that kept women safely isolated from the outside world, lest they be somehow tainted. She came from a similar place, but had obviously been inspired by the Scottish grandmother she spoke about so reverently.

Emad wondered if he would be allowed to meet Olivia MacQuaid one of these days. Likely *required*. He presumed that her approval would be even more important than Zareen's father Nigel, at the end of the day.

Time passed. Two vehicles came into sight in the distance, taking the main road into town, one a luxury beast where the Frenchman had boarded and the other a truck carrying several trunks, presumably clothing and supplies for the Germans, as well as the flight crew for the aircraft, and presumably the assassin Bertrand.

"That is them," Asher spoke over the wind-blown silence, confirming things, so Emad started the Ford and slipped it noisily into gear.

They returned to the main road and Emad concentrated on the area in front of him, wondering when he would encounter the remainder of the men from Bughra's compound. And if a firefight would ensue.

If Hans or Finn were here, they could possibly even steal the other Heinkel right now, just to strand the Germans in Samarkand and elude them until such time as Zareen could disappear into the Tibetan Plateau, but that would not be possible today.

He pulled into the area of the airstrip, passing a wire fence designed to keep stray camels from wandering out into the way of planes landing and taking off. There was a Quonset hut down a ways, and Emad could see people resting in the shade, so he drove closer.

Men rose as the truck approached, so he hoped that everyone with him was paying attention. Looking closer as he got there, the men were not visibly armed, which made sense if a group of German diplomats had just arrived.

Emad wondered what story these men had given the Germans. Perhaps the pilot needed to go into town to get someone to bring fuel? This was not a bustling place with dozens of aircraft and a variety of services immediately available. At least town wasn't that far away.

On the other hand, that would mean that the Germans would be returning soon. At least the flight crew. Possibly all of them, if anyone local had heard about Captain Bughra.

Emad had a smile at the thought of the Frenchman and his compatriots rushing to the compound he had just left. Presumably, Zareen and Ghada had left enough guns behind, once those men managed to get themselves untied from Asher's ministrations.

How long did they have before everyone converged angrily on this airstrip?

Finn and the others would presumably be returning from Kashgar in less than two hours, if he had understood the timing of the thing. Should he take the time to disable the German plane, or prepare to steal it?

He would ask the woman in charge, once she had taken in a new set of prisoners.

Emad calculated his distance and punched the clutch in, swerving a little wide as he got close and Zareen leaned out the window with a machine pistol firmly pointed at the nearest man.

"Would you like to surrender to me, or does your honor demand that you die in battle right now?" Ghada asked from the bed in a loud voice.

A deadly voice.

A woman with about as much compunction on the topic as killing and cleaning a chicken for dinner.

Emad had always prided himself on being a hard man, willing to be ruthless in pursuit of his war against the Italians. Against his men and his foes, he had excelled.

Ghada Attar probably considered him an enthusiastic puppy by comparison. Emad was not sure she was wrong.

He could, however, learn.

Emad set the emergency brake and hopped out on his side when it became clear that these men weren't *that* fanatical about their task. Quickly, he and Asher got them disarmed and moved into the shade again.

The Quonset hut held a small private plane of some sort, so Asher tied the six men up with some rope inside and Emad moved the truck where it could not be seen from the road approaching. You would need to be within about fifty yards of the place to notice the vehicle. That should give them time to prepare an ambush.

Asher stopped and cocked his head in a most human manner. Emad concentrated on the prisoners, but listened to the quiet conversation.

"What is it?" Zareen asked.

"The California Condor is returning," Asher replied.

CHAPTER TWENTY-NINE

Finn studied the horizon as he started his long approach into Samarkand and that little strip clear out on the north edge of town he'd been at before. Hans was in back, watching Bughra, but the guy was trussed like a Christmas ham at this point by a grumpy Kraut, so Finn was alone with his thoughts.

And his troubles.

Shit.

Even from here he recognized the lines on the beast. Similar to his, before some friends of friends had done things to the Condor to make her not look so much like that Heinkel H-111 sitting on the side of the field.

The one with big, ugly swastika on the tail.

Even on his best day, Finn was in possession of stolen goods. To wit: an aircraft supposedly sold by the German government to the Chinese nationalists. Given the complicated trigonometry of politics in this region, Finn was willing to bet that the Nazis would be supporting those Chinese Nationalist Army against the Communists, with the Russians across the battle-field by proxy.

Shit.

Fuel tanks weren't dry, but he hadn't stopped at Osh to

refill, much as that might have been a smart idea. But then he'd have had to explain to them folk about a stolen aircraft as well.

Airstrip looked abandoned, but Finn wasn't beguiled. He did a full orbit at about one thousand feet, spotting an old flatbed parked out of sight behind a Quonset hut.

Then somebody walked out from the building and waved. Too high to see who it was, but they knew him. Desert robes suggested Asher. A second figure emerged a moment later and cast a smaller shadow in a way that suggested Zareen.

Might be a trap, but whoever it was only had small arms, and Finn was in a flying pillbox with a lot of machine guns.

"Hans, haul your ass up here," he yelled over his shoulder.

The big Kraut was there a moment later.

"I saw," he said. "Ventral guns would be useful. Or dorsal. If you roll up normally, I can be in the starboard gun and you can man the nose cannons as soon as you stop. It would be useful if your nose machine guns were lined up with the other plane, just in case."

"That works," Finn said. "How's our guest?"

"Somebody rang his bell," Hans laughed. "A few times. He is still a little groggy, but none the worse for the wear. A bit grumpy, though."

"Nothing time won't heal," Finn growled. "Okay, stand by for landing. Coming in hot, just in case."

Hans vanished and Finn went to automatic, scanning the skies around him for trouble, but not seeing any. Downwind was clear, baseline was safe, so he went to final approach, landing a little longer than he might have normally and leaving things too fast on the ground until he would have gotten a chewing-out in Tehran or Chicago and maybe gotten his license suspended.

Didn't care here.

He finally shut it down and coasted to a stop, feathering the propellers instead of killing the engines. Brake set, he shifted forward, in case he needed to hose the other Heinkel down with lead. From this range, shooting fish in a barrel.

Zareen approached from the front where he could see her. She had a Russian submachinegun on her hip, so he popped open a window to talk.

"Where is Bughra?" she called.

"Hans has him tied up in back," Finn replied. "What's going on?"

"We've escaped, for now," she yelled. "But time is critical, as you can guess."

She gestured back over her shoulder at the other plane and Finn grimaced.

Still, she seemed to be in control, so he shut the engines down. Asher emerged and set chocks under the wheels for the moment. Emad was standing in a doorway, so maybe he was guarding the punks that had been here before.

Quickly, Finn and Hans got their prisoner out and added to the mix as Zareen gave him a quick rundown.

"Ghada did what?" Finn interrupted at one point.

"It worked, Finn," Zareen said. "We took them all prisoner, then came here and surprised these men as well."

"I assume the German flight crew will return shortly with a fuel truck," Finn said. "We cannot hide the Condor, so we will need to capture those men and get our aircraft refueled. Meanwhile, let us get all of our luggage and supplies aboard, so we are ready to leave as soon as we can."

Folks nodded and got to work. Finn went in to check the prisoners. He knelt down in front of Bughra.

"Sorry about all that," Finn said to the man.

Bughra shrugged. At least his color was returning to normal.

"Fortunes of war," the man said. "I took your party prisoner, but tried to be polite. It paid off, because you've taken me prisoner now, instead of killing everyone. Where did the bombs go?"

"I dropped them on the Russian side of the mountains, as far away from everyone as I could. Not in the mood to commit war crimes or declare war on anybody right this moment."

"I understand," Bughra nodded. "But I will talk to my superiors about building an air force that might allow us to retake Kashgar and drive the Chinese and their allies out."

"Maybe you'll get lucky, then, and can steal the other bomber when I'm gone," Finn laughed. "It's close enough to mine. You'll just need a pilot you trust."

"Yes, that would be wise," Captain Bughra laughed as well.

"Finn," Zareen interrupted. "Company."

He glanced over and rose, pausing to look back.

"You stay low, in case there's any shooting, okay?" he asked the guy.

Finn didn't bother waiting for a response as he moved to the door.

CHAPTER THIRTY

Zareen had never imagined that her world would turn into one where she needed a machine gun. Two years ago, it had been libraries and tea rooms. Now she was standing just inside the doorway of a Quonset hut in Soviet Central Asia, watching over Ghada's shoulder through the mostly closed door as they prepared to ambush a group of complete strangers.

At least she could place most, if not all, of the blame for this at the feet of Didier Beauchêne. Even when he had access to his assassin, Bertrand, they had never come to violence. Not until Cairo. Not until it became clear that she had stolen a march on the Frenchman and stood poised to learn something that would change the world.

Thus fascism. It would not share with the world. It conquered and applied a boot to the neck to get its way.

Zareen was aware of Emad's smell and his heat, standing directly behind her, almost touching but somehow keeping a perfect distance away. She could turn around right now and perhaps kiss the man without moving, but it would no doubt shock him beyond all rational thought at a moment when she needed the warrior ready.

They would have that conversation soon, though.

A vehicle approached, noisily downshifting gears then braking. She heard someone exclaim surprise in German, which she assumed was the pilot of the new aircraft. Ghada tensed, so Zareen did as well, presuming that the ambush was about to spring.

Outside, the truck came to a halt and the engine died. Ghada threw the door open and surged out, her own machine pistol centered. She did not speak, but ran on silent feet.

The passenger was facing Zareen when he got out of the vehicle, stopping to goggle in surprise as she moved close and pointed her gun at the man. From the corner of her eye, she could see Ghada do the same to the driver, and Emad came to rest covering the front of the truck.

"*Was ist das?*" the passenger asked.

He was dressed like a German Luftwaffe officer, in gray tunic and pants. No gun, so he was not apparently tempted to do anything. Perhaps thirty years old, with blond hair cropped short under a short-billed forage cap.

"You are my prisoner," Zareen told the man casually in German. The gun pointed at his mid-section, and all the armed men accompanying her, made her point rather emphatically.

He put his hands up, as did the man who had been sitting in the center of the vehicle.

Ghada got them all lined up by the side of the vehicle as Finn moved the truck over by the Condor.

Asher emerged and escorted everyone inside, where he would tie them up as expertly as he had the others. Zareen had herself a menagerie now, but she wouldn't be staying long. They needed to be gone from Samarkand as fast as they could refuel the craft, although she wasn't going to be paying for this, so she supposed that it would just add to her legend.

What had Finn called them? Air Pirates of Cyrenaica? Yes, that had a nice ring to it. Perhaps she needed to have little logos sewn, so they could have cute uniforms to go into battle, or something equally silly.

Zareen found herself alone with Finn. Hans was getting the fuel tanks on the Condor filled. Ghada and Emad had escorted the new prisoners inside.

"How did it go?" she asked.

They hadn't had much chance to talk since he got back.

"Snuck up on the man and ambushed him," Finn said in a serious tone. "Kinda like all this. Didn't need to kill him, and he didn't do anything stupid. And Ghada took them all prisoner back at the compound by herself?"

"She did," Zareen smiled. "It was a most wicked trick to play on those men, but it was her idea. I would have never imagined doing something similar. Then we came to rescue you, unaware that the others had been following us. A few hours later and they might have landed right on top of us. Had they flown overnight, they might have been here this morning to capture you before you took off."

"Willing to run with that kind of luck," Finn said. "Dropped the bombs safely in Russia somewhere, so the Chinese won't be too pissed at us when we come through. What do we do about the Condor? It's obvious now what it is. And the Germans can wire ahead and tell people we're in a stolen plane."

"Only if they knew where we are going," Zareen said. "I would suggest someplace like Kabul, but Afghanistan is still recovering from their turbulence over the last two decades, and I fear we might not be able to get what we need. Can you make it to Lahore, in British India?"

She was always amazed by the way the man seemed to have a complete map of the globe in his head, able to estimate directions and distances to any location she mentioned, even before he needed to consult something so prosaic as paper.

"One way?" he asked. She nodded. "Piece of cake. About eleven hundred kilometers, so about a half-tank of gas. Why?"

"The British are more likely to ignore a German demand than a local tribal elder elevated to king or shah, Finn," Zareen explained. "Plus, I can make certain things known to a British officer, were it to come to that. But I agree, the time of the California Condor is probably already passed, sad as it makes me, and we need to locate a new aircraft. Something capable of long distances and hauling significant cargo."

"Then you probably want one of the new Douglas DC-2s, Zareen," he replied. "Or the newer DC-3. About the same speed and range, but capable of hauling a lot of people. I've even read about sleeper versions configured like train cars, for people crossing the country overnight."

"Good, I will let you and Hans go about finding us something, and I think we need to head to Lahore."

"Also puts us in a position to cross northern India to where we're going," Finn agreed.

Zareen smiled. That was why she had recruited the two men. They were experts at making things happen, even when her plans had to change radically. She could rely on Finn and Hans, and Emad, to roll with the punches and still come out swinging.

"How long until the Condor is ready to fly?" she asked after a few moments of silence.

"Not long," Finn nodded. "Normally, we'd pull some maintenance, but I can see just flying into the sunset right now, and then getting through Afghanistan and across the Khyber Pass. Think we can elude them?"

"If I trusted our reception in Kashgar, I would have asked you to repeat today's flight," Zareen grimaced some. "But Didier Beauchêne with German allies make things more complicated, so we need to elude them. I had considered suggesting Almaty, in Soviet Kazakhstan, but I agree that we need to acquire a different aircraft before we do anything else, and Lahore keeps us closer to our goal."

Finn turned and looked past her shoulder now with surprise on his face.

"Hans, we just ran out of time!" he exclaimed. "How close are you?"

"Close enough," the German called back, looking around wildly. "What happened?"

"Bad guys are coming from town," Finn yelled. He turned to her. "Get everyone loaded right now. We have to leave."

Zareen turned and saw a dust cloud in the distance, slowly closing. She wasn't sure why Finn thought it was Didier, but she wasn't going to argue with the man.

"Ghada, bring the others," she yelled in turn, trailing Finn in the direction of the aircraft. A glance back confirmed that the others had followed.

He climbed into the aircraft and headed forward. Zareen went to the bench just behind the cockpit and began to strap herself in. Emad was first to board, so she flagged him down.

"Take one of the side guns, Emad," she ordered. "Be prepared to fire on whoever has arrived, but you are not required to kill anyone."

Murder in Soviet territory would not look good, if she ever wanted to return. Finn had talked vaguely about his reasons for never returning to the United States, but cold-blooded murder was one of the few charges he was not facing, apparently.

Emad paused, then nodded and took up a position on the side, charging the weapon and rotating it once to check things. The interior had been modified from the bomber version by adding seats and removing many of the armor plates. The overhead gun was now fired by standing on a shelf that was deployed out, so that might be a problem. Similarly, the two guns firing down required you to open a plate in the floor to access them.

Using the side gun let him be out of the way as Ghada and Asher climbed aboard. Hans had not joined them, even as the engines started up with a roar and a vibration she felt clear to her marrow.

The Germans, if it was them, must be getting close.

Would they be fast enough to escape?

CHAPTER THIRTY-ONE

Finn checked everything. Helped that the aircraft was still pretty warm, having only sat for about twenty minutes. He was about to start the engines, but Hans had taken his time about disconnecting the hose.

Finn opened the side window as the big Kraut finally disconnected things and seemed intent on walking instead of running.

"Would you get your ass in gear?" Finn yelled out the side window.

Didn't help that he could see the car turning into the airstrip now, right in front of him the way that he had parked the Condor earlier.

Then the stupid Kraut walked, no *ambled*, over to the other plane, like he was giving it an inspection or something.

Up there, that big staff car was pointed this way. From the way they were throwing dust and sand into the air, the driver had downshifted and was trying to cut him off or something. Stupid, considering that Finn still had all the guns this bird came equipped with, including the one forward where Hans might shoot at them.

If he would ever get off his ass so they could leave.

A sound snapped Finn's head around.

That was a gunshot, but from the side.

A second gunshot.

The German plane twanged sharply, and Hans finally started running.

From the look on his face, Finn's co-pilot and chief trouble-maker was also laughing, but he couldn't hear it over the engines.

Finn waited, counting the steps and seconds as Hans disappeared around the wing.

A solid thump aft and the interior door opened.

"He's aboard," Zareen yelled.

Go.

Finn popped the brakes and pushed the throttle forward. They had three-quarters of a load of fuel. More than enough to get where he was going, since he had no intention of returning to Samarkand.

The California Condor began to roll.

CHAPTER THIRTY-TWO

Didier had only just settled in his hotel room when there was a rap at the door. He kept his grumbles under his breath, because Bertrand did not sound like that.

Given the options, he was hoping that Konrad had something he had forgotten earlier, but Didier didn't get his hopes up. He opened the door and stared at the woman, thinking that his luggage had not even arrived from the second vehicle.

"*Fraulein*?" he asked, having apparently finally reached the end of the evasions that would keep the woman at bay.

"We're leaving, Beauchêne," she said curtly. "Come with me."

Rather than await an answer, the damnable woman reached in and grabbed him by the lapel, dragging Didier out into the hallway as he squawked in surprise.

"What is going on?" he demanded, but she turned him to the right and pushed.

It was not enough of a shove to topple him, but Didier stumbled several steps. Reiher was right on his heels and hooked her arm in his elbow, compelling him forward with a smile on her face that left him even colder, if that was possible.

"They have been spotted," she announced as they reached the end of the hallway and down the stairs to the lobby.

"Who?" he asked blankly.

"Shirazi," Fraulein Reiher announced triumphantly. "Here, in Samarkand."

"What are you talking about?" Didier managed to get his feet under him now, as the tall woman used her long legs to speed up.

Konrad was standing just inside the front door of the lobby. He turned and exited as soon as they came into sight.

"They arrived yesterday," the tall blonde bombshell announced as she hurried him forward. "The aircraft departed at first light this morning, but watchers have seen it just now, returning from the southeast. It appears to be flying back to the landing strip where our aircraft is parked, so we must hurry and intercept them."

A car pulled up and Konrad climbed in. Apparently, Reiher distrusted Didier's motives, because she thrust him into the back and then got in, trapping him between the two Germans as the car sped away.

"They have returned?" Didier turned to Konrad instead.

Any excuse to keep some physical and social distance from the woman even now pressing her chest against his arm.

"One of our agents contacted me as soon as we arrived at the hotel," Konrad explained. "There is some confusion, as they checked in yesterday at this very same hotel, but then checked out in an emergency just a few hours later. However, the aircraft remained present until this morning. And spotters noticed it a few minutes ago, returning. We have them now."

Didier held his opinion on that topic. Zareen Shirazi had proven to be a worthwhile opponent. He doubted that it would be so simple.

Something must have shown on his face. Konrad's elation suddenly turned dour.

"What?" the man demanded.

Didier sought for a moment to find the right words. He still needed the Germans, at least for now. Doubly so if they might actually succeed, however accidentally it was.

"Were it just Shirazi, I might have greater confidence," Didier began carefully. "But she has recruited several capable men to her small army, including the pilots of the aircraft she hired to take her into the desert, one of whom was apparently previously an American gangster of some sort. At some point, she also recruited a Libyan Senussi warrior from the deep desert, connected to the Court of Idris. Plus, spotters suggest the Man With No Face is now part of her company."

He paused to take a breath.

"I think you risk underestimating them, as you are confronting the woman and her assistants by yourselves. You did not even think to bring Bertrand with us, even though the man is a competent killer in his own right."

Somehow, Didier was not surprised when both Konrad and the Fraulein pulled Luger pistols from holsters, as if to show off. But he was just along as a companion here, overruled by the German High Command on any opinion he might choose to have, so he subsided, without even a grumble.

They would see the truth for themselves. Perhaps it would even go so far as to puncture some of their Teutonic pomposity.

At least he would be able to say he warned them, if it became necessary later.

The ride itself was not long. Samarkand, for having been the capital at one time, was still a relatively small town. The driver said something and Didier leaned forward.

Being in the middle seat gave him an unobstructed view.

Two bombers, similar in lines, side by side. Neither was original, but modifications in the field had moved them different directions. But there was no doubting that they had indeed spotted their prey.

"They are getting away," the driver suddenly called.

"Faster," Reiher snarled. "Catch them."

Didier had his doubts about catching an aircraft, but again, he subsided rather than argue with an entire menagerie of fools.

Fraulein Reiher went so far as to roll her window down and climb halfway out to fire.

That left him with an unfortunate view of the woman's bottom. He supposed it wasn't bad, if much broader than attractive. Perhaps he could maintain such an image the next time she knocked on his door.

Konrad, that dry scholar of a man, did the same, rolling his window down and firing his pitiful pistol.

Didier looked both ways, then braced himself against the back of the seat in front of him. The best these two fools could do would be to anger Shirazi and her companions right now.

And someone succeeded. The sound was like metal tearing. It took Didier a moment to realize that the aircraft had opened fire on their car with machine guns.

He made himself as small as possible as the car began to shudder violently and swerve.

A sudden scream, and *Fraulein* Reiher disappeared out the window before he could grab a boot.

A moment later and the car suddenly jerked to the right, throwing Konrad out as well.

The vehicle began to drift at high speed. Didier realized that the driver was dead and the car out of control. He braced, but there were no trees or ditches, so perhaps it would merely roll to a stop. In the distance, he heard the aircraft's engines roar like an angry dragon, and then he watched it begin to accelerate, racing right past them the other direction.

The car's engine finally stalled as the stolen bomber achieved flight, and Didier climbed out the passenger side, unwilling to get too close to the dead body of the driver.

He turned to watch his enemy escape and miraculously both Konrad and the *Fraulein* were standing, covered in dust, having been simply thrown clear by the erratic maneuvering.

He began to walk that way, meeting Konrad first.

"Congratulations," Dr. Schwarzenberg said as Didier got close to the man.

"I beg your pardon?" Didier said, surprised.

"You were right, Didier," the man said in a disgusted tone.

Didier shrugged. He had been at this game far longer than these two, blundering amateurs.

Perhaps he could control them, yet.

CHAPTER THIRTY-THREE

Zareen breathed a sigh of relief when the wheels left the ground. Hans and Emad both hammering away on the guns had concerned her, but they had apparently escaped whatever was happening back there.

"How soon until they can pursue us?" she asked Hans.

The man grinned at her as he locked the machine gun in place.

"Not until they repair the two tires on their aircraft that I shot out before we left," he laughed. "If they are incredibly lucky, tomorrow. If I damaged a wheel or an axle, they might be a week."

The others smiled as well.

Zareen unbuckled and rose, gesturing Hans and Emad to sit with Ghada and Asher.

"I need to talk to Finn about our destination," she said.

They nodded and she moved to the cockpit.

Finn was also grinning when she got there, so she moved to the forward seat and turned sideways to watch the man.

He watched her in return.

"Lahore?" he asked.

"Yes, but I need you to fly northeast for now, until we are

out of sight," she called over the sound. "As if we are headed to Bishkek or Almaty."

"What's up there that would mislead them?" Finn asked.

"There is a place in distant Siberia," Zareen explained. "Tunguska. In 1908, there was an explosion similar to the one that stranded Asher in Egypt a decade later."

"Really?"

"Hundreds of square kilometers of forest leveled by a low-altitude explosive wave," Zareen said. "Nobody has scientifically explored it that I am aware of, because it took so long for the news to trickle out of Imperial Russia, and then the various wars intruded. Finally, Stalin closed the borders. But if we can convince Didier that we are headed to Siberia, at the least we gain a few more days lead on him until we can get into Tibet for our goal."

"You're the boss," he replied, starting a smooth turn.

Zareen leaned into the turn and watched the sky move around. She thought for a few minutes until she found the words she sought.

"You are not attached to any one aircraft, are you?" she finally asked. "So much as the concept of flying."

He shrugged and chewed on his words, but Finn was like that much of the time. Reticent. Cognizant of things around him, but slow to comment unless asked.

"I wanna fly," he finally admitted. "But yeah, don't really care in what. This was always a stolen car and we were just waiting for a BOLO."

"Bolo?"

"*Be On the Look Out*," Finn grinned at her. "Cop term from the States."

"Ah," she said. "Well, next time I hope we can buy a legitimate aircraft. I like your thought of a cargo carrier. It will allow you to perhaps make some money of your own on the side, while I continue to pay you and Hans to ferry me all over the world."

"Not you really paying," Finn replied obliquely.

"That is true, Finn," Zareen admitted. "But I feel that I must bring you into a deeper conspiracy now. And Hans as well, but I doubt he would care all that much, one way or the other."

"Okay."

That was all he said. One word, but it summed up everything she liked and respected about the man. He would do what he thought was right, and as long as he thought she was on that track, he would go along. If she deviated, he would say something.

Or not. Finn Severijns could be as stubborn as Zareen Shirazi. He might decide to simply leave, rather than argue with her.

She would have to make sure it never came to that. If nothing else, he made a most excellent moral compass. Zareen suspected that she would need something like that as she got deeper into her own secret plans.

"I was speaking with Emad earlier," she began. "He has deduced my long-term plan."

"Sure," Finn nodded. "Kick out the Russians and the Brits. Keep the Americans and Japanese from walking in instead. Give birth to a new Parthian Empire. They were successful the longest."

His words took her breath away. His grin spoke volumes.

"If the Canadians crossed south, or more Mexicans like Pancho Villa came north, I'd be the same way, Zareen," he said. "It's your homeland. One of them, anyway, and the world's been arguing over it for thousands of years. Now you got oil, so everybody wants to control that and won't leave you alone. We just left what the Russians have been doing to Central Asia and you want to stop them cold from pushing all the way to the Persian Gulf or the Indian Ocean."

"And you support this?" she asked.

"I support you," he corrected her. "If you succeed, Persia

maybe turns into a nice, peaceful place and kind of anchors everybody on all sides of you, which would be better for most of the world and the Brits can go pound sand for all I care."

"The Americans might not agree," she suggested as a new tack.

"When I can safely return home without getting arrested, maybe we'll worry about that, but I don't see that happening anytime soon," he grimaced. "Until then, you hired me and Hans to fly you around, and you're still a partner in this air company, since you put money into buying it."

"Partners?" she asked.

Zareen hadn't really considered it in those terms.

"Partners," Finn nodded. "And you're the managing partner, because you'll listen to the rest of us if we have an idea or complaint, but this is your mission."

"Even now?"

"Now we're going to fly across the top of the world, Zareen," Finn said. "Maybe over it, depending on how you want to measure those things. Asher will take us to a place and we'll maybe get one or two steps closer to saving the world from those silly madmen in Rome and Berlin."

"And London and D.C.?" she pressed.

"Especially those fools," he agreed.

Zareen nodded. Surprised, but content. She could work with this, and it helped, knowing that she had a full team, and they were all on board with her.

She rose.

"Thank you, Finn," she said, and he just grinned at her.

"Could you send Hans forward when you get there?" he asked. "We need to calculate a lot of things and didn't exactly take the time to plot all this out before we left."

"I will," she agreed, heading aft.

She and Hans traded places and she smiled at Ghada next to her and Emad and Asher across the way.

"There will be a slight detour," she announced. "We will fly through British Raj India for a brief stop, I hope, and then Asher, we will see what the Durren have left us."

"What do you hope to find, Zareen?" Asher asked.

She paused, looking for the right words.

"Tomorrow," she replied.

READ MORE!

Be sure to read all the books in the Air Pirates of Cyrenaica series!
https://www.knottedroadpress.com/product-category/science-fiction/air-pirates-of-cyrenaica/

ABOUT THE AUTHOR

Blaze Ward writes science fiction in the Alexandria Station universe (Jessica Keller, The Science Officer, Phil Kosnett, etc.) as well as several other science fiction universes, such as Corsac Fox, Operation Marrakesh, and more. He also writes odd bits of high fantasy with swords and orcs. In addition, he is the Editor and Publisher of *Boundary Shock Quarterly Magazine*. You can find out more at his website www.blazeward.com, as well as Facebook, Goodreads, and other places.

Blaze's works are available as ebooks, paper, and audio, and can be found at a variety of online vendors. His newsletter comes out regularly, and you can also follow his blog on his website. He really enjoys interacting with fans, and looks forward to any and all questions—even ones about his books!

Never miss a release!
If you'd like to be notified of new releases, sign up for my newsletter.

http://www.blazeward.com/newsletter/

Buy More!
Did you know that you can buy directly from the KRP website?

https://www.knottedroadpress.com/shop/

Connect with Blaze!

Web: www.blazeward.com
Boundary Shock Quarterly (BSQ):
https://www.boundaryshockquarterly.com/

ABOUT KNOTTED ROAD PRESS

Knotted Road Press publishes dynamic fiction set in exotic locations and unique non-fiction voices in genres such as autobiography, business, cookbooks, and how-to. Our authors cover a wide range of genres including science fiction, fantasy, mystery, literary, and poetry, appealing to all readers. We offer both DRM-free ebooks and print books for a global readership.

Knotted Road Press
www.KnottedRoadPress.com
www.KnottedRoadPress.com/Shop